Butterscotch Moon

Susan Kirby

Forever Romances

is an imprint of
Guideposts Associates, Inc.
Carmel, NY 10512

This Guideposts edition is published by special arrangement with Susan Kirby.

Chapter One

Natalie Franklin absorbed the panorama of rolling hills dotted with vibrant green grass, spring wildflowers, and outcroppings of rock. Her eyes feasted on fields set at jaunty angles to defy the rugged terrain, orchards in blossom, hills too rocky for farming shin-high in grasses, and farm buildings clustered in valleys or clinging to hills. Fuzzy-faced calves frisked in sun-warmed meadows, and a ground squirrel darted for the safety of roadside undergrowth as Natalie's blue Pinto whisked by.

It was still Illinois, yet one hundred fifty miles in a southerly direction made a difference. The hills thrilled her most. Such rolling green splendor beneath a cobalt blue sky! And it was almost spring.

Spring! The season of beginnings! Natalie's optimism surfaced in a glorious smile, for she, too, was making a fresh beginning. She had answered an ad in *Gleanings,* a genealogical pamphlet, and landed an interview for a guaranteed-to-pay writing job.

Her thoughts returned to the road and she realized her speed had dropped as her mind wandered. In her sideview mirror she caught a glimpse of a car edging out to pass on the narrow two-lane highway, then falling in behind her again as they approached a blind curve. Her sudden burst of speed had kept the driver from passing. She thought with chagrin of her brothers' accusations that she drove as she walked—taking running skips to make up for dawdling.

Perhaps it was a fair observation. She and the bright red TransAm had hopscotched for the past fifty miles, passing and being passed in turn.

Her rearview mirror threw her the reflection of the lone occupant of the red car. He was youngish, tall in the seat, and had dark and wavy hair. His cheeks were ripe for a shave, and his sturdy, angular chin was faintly cleft.

Finding himself the object of her less-than-discreet study, the man uncurled two fingers from the steering wheel and wagged them at her. Natalie jerked her gaze away from the mirror, riveting her attention on the road where it belonged. Presently, she laughed. That mocking wave served her right. She shouldn't have shot ahead of him like that when he was trying to pass.

Presently, the red car sped past as she slowed to read a sign. The next turn ought to be hers. Ahead of her the TransAm slowed and made the same turn she was to make.

Once off the main highway, Natalie paid closer attention to the hand-drawn map Mrs. Brandon had sent her. Spotting the Shell station to which the instructions referred, she made a left turn onto a paved county road. Just as she turned, she noticed the red sports car had stopped at the station. The driver was out stretching long legs and shrugging the kinks out of a set of wide shoulders.

Dark curly hair tumbled down roguishly to dust a

high, intelligent brow. The darkness of hair was repeated in a slash of thick brows and again in a generous mustache beneath a broad, well-shaped nose. He was squinting against the sun. Even the squint seemed attractive, for there was a stamp of character on his craggy features and a suggestion of dimples beneath the razor stubble.

The short sleeves of the man's pink knit shirt revealed tanned forearms; his shirttail was tucked into a pair of white trousers. Conscious of the statements made by color, Natalie slowed even more, her feminine interest stirred. Pink on this man meant he was confident enough of his masculinity not to worry that a color was traditionally feminine.

A sharp blast of horn jerked her to attention. She'd been thoughtlessly taking her half of the road out of the middle. She steered into the proper lane with a little burst of speed, and a pickup truck barreled by with a wizened old man working his mouth and shaking one fist out the window.

The man in the pink shirt grinned at her—she'd been right about the dimples—and gave her another two-fingered salute.

Two or three miles down the road her face finally cooled, and then only because she'd lowered her window. The rush of air whipped baby-fine brown hair off her shoulders and steadied her nerves. If there were guardian angels, and she chose to believe there were, she was overtaxing hers today. "Keep your mind on the road, Nat!" she muttered in a scolding tone.

The Sutton house was an impressive structure, at the end of a leisurely loop of lane. The bricks were softened to a rose hue and a colonnaded porch stretched across the front of the two-and-a-half story structure. On one end of the house, the roof rose steeply to a tower that reminded Nat of the castles and moats and drawbridges of storybook days.

Snugly nestled by old trees, manicured bushes, and colorful spring flowers, the place had an atmosphere of friendly warmth. A wooden swing hung from the branch of a widespread oak, and near the porch steps, a child's bicycle was parked in a state of waiting, as if the child had just run in for a drink and a cookie and would soon return to play.

With a prayer in her heart, Natalie reached for the brass knocker. When it proved to be ornamental, she pressed the doorbell, then waited. A small pinch-mouthed woman swung open the door and peered at her with sharp black eyes.

"May I help you?"

"I'm Natalie Franklin. I have an interview with Mrs. Brandon at eleven," she said, tucking her insecurities behind a friendly smile.

The woman conducted a visual inspection. Nat returned her silent study, mentally naming her "the lady in gray." Her charcoal-colored hair, her dress, and her stockings all were gray.

"I guess you're the one come to see about Marianne's book whimsy," the woman said at last. "A great to-do about nothing, if you ask me. But she's got this bee in her bonnet, and there's no stopping her.

"If there was, Harold would have done it by now." The housekeeper continued her monologue as she led the way through a spacious hallway into a charming parlor. "It's all tangled up with his campaign, you know. Though what makes him think the news media'll pick up on something as boring as the Sutton family history, I don't know. Harold's all too quick to jump at shadows, if you know what I mean."

Natalie hadn't the faintest idea what she meant, nor was she inclined to inquire.

The parlor was unoccupied. Natalie ventured, "I believe I'm right on time. Is Mrs. Brandon ready to see me?"

The housekeeper rolled her dark eyes. "I doubt it. She's got her hands full with Harold right now, off in the library there." She gestured toward a closed door at the far end of the parlor. "Could be he's still trying to talk her out of this book idea. If he is, he's wasting his breath. But then Harold's got a good supply of that to waste. I'll bring you coffee. Oh, don't sit in that chair; it has a weak leg."

Wondering what she'd walked into, Natalie moved to the sofa. The woman obviously had no qualms about sharing her opinions of the family. And in such a way as to surround Nat with a cloud of confusion.

Who was Harold and why did he object to publishing a family history? Nat was suddenly beset by misgivings. The job had seemed perfectly fitted to her needs only minutes ago.

To dismiss an attack of nerves, she scanned the room with admiration. The natural beauty of the wood floor was complemented by rich red brown Moroccan rugs alive with geometric designs of pale yellow, burgundy, mauve, and deep chocolate. The walls, the upholstered pieces, the draperies, and even the stone fireplace were a muted eggshell. The dark wood of the antique chair the woman had warned Natalie from and a pair of marble-top rosewood tables echoed the chocolate tones in the rugs. A bouquet of golden tulips graced a grand piano, picking out accents of gold in the carpets as did the brass fireplace accessories.

All in all, the room inspired trust. Nat had nearly dismissed the woman's prattling as irrelevant when the coffee was delivered.

"Thank you. Coffee smells marvelous after my long drive." Natalie accepted the cup with genuine appreciation and with her free hand made an all-encompassing gesture. "What a beautiful room. Are the older pieces original to the house?"

"Very few of them, actually," the housekeeper confided. "Jacob Sutton made a fortune from the local salt springs. He built this house in the 1830s and furnished it with the best. But after the Civil War the family fell on hard times and had to sell most of the valuable pieces.

"The family did keep the house, though. Then, around the turn of the century Marianne's grandfather fixed the house up again. He married money, you see, and made quite a bundle himself in some mines to the west. He spent a sinful amount collecting furniture from all over the world." She pointed a bony finger. "That chair I told you not to sit in? It came from France. The lion faces on the arm rests are hand-carved."

"It's certainly an interesting house and plainly rich in history, too, Mrs..."

"I'm Hannah. Hannah Simon. And there's no need dressing it up with 'Mrs.' My mister's been dead for twenty years. Now you sit right there, Missy. Don't be poking around stirring up dust. Marianne'll get to you as soon as she can."

Hannah whirled around and tramped off, her dress whipping at broomstick-thin legs. Natalie let out a small sigh and tapped her foot nervously.

The coffee was strong and black and hot, the kind her brothers used to tease about—"Watch it, Nat; that'll put hair on your chest." She smiled into her cup, thinking of her five brothers. They'd been a puzzle of contradictions—bullying one minute, protecting the next; tattling over some small misdeed, covering up another; horse-laughing at her slips of the tongue, lashing out at anyone else who made her cry.

All in all, they'd taught her not to take herself too seriously and at the same time to be assertive in a firm but gentle way. And because their small home had always been overrun with boys, she knew boys could be just as bewildered by girls as girls were by boys. The discovery had served her well. Few men made her uncomfortable, and those who did didn't manage it for long. She made friends with men easily.

And that was the way she wanted it. She had too much to do with her life to fall in love.

From behind the closed library door came a sudden angry shout. Nat jumped and jostled her coffee cup as she tried to fit it to the saucer on the marble-top table. The second much quieter exclamation was her own, for though she had managed to keep the fragile cup from crashing to the floor, the coffee was running across the rosewood table toward the Moroccan rug.

Diving a hand into her pocketbook, she came up with a wad of tissues. They absorbed the spill before it could drip to the rug, but she was left with a handful of soppy tissues and nowhere to put them. There certainly weren't any trash containers in full view.

She started to toss them back into her purse, but the purse was new and too great a sacrifice for an awkward moment. She considered looking for Hannah or

11

at least a wastepaper basket in another room, but her instructions to sit tight kept her from wandering.

With a writer's eye for the ridiculous, she visualized herself sauntering into the library with a wet wad of tissues only to have Mrs. Brandon extend her hand in greeting.

That image brought her to her feet in a hurry. Going to the nearest window, she held the tissues well away from her skirt and tried with her free hand to shove open the window. As she exerted a little more muscle against the stubborn window, her conscience nagged her. But good grief, what else was she to do? After her interview was over, she could slip around the bushes there and pick up the wet glob.

Drat! The thing wouldn't open. She grunted softly, giving it one last try.

Jacob Brandon let himself into the house, thinking that for all the good the trip had done he might as well have stayed home. He rubbed his eyes, gritty from the all-night drive, and yawned. Maybe after some lunch and a hot shower he'd regain his perspective on the project.

Before he reached the stairs, he stopped short at the sound of Harold's voice raised in anger. *What now?* he thought. An old familiar weariness compounded the weight of a sleepless night as he heard his mother's calming voice muted by the library door.

He yawned again, determined not to investigate the cause of all the yelling. He would have gone on up to his room but a smothered exclamation of distress alerted him that he wasn't alone.

A young woman was in the parlor sopping up a cup of spilled coffee. Unaware of his presence, she rose to

12

her feet and glanced around the room. He watched her hesitate and cross to the nearest window and with the soft sound of exertion try to lift it.

It was the woman in the blue Pinto, of course. He'd spotted her car in the drive and stared curiously, then drawn the obvious conclusion: a representative from some political group had come to feel Harold out on the issues.

However jaded Jacob was to politics in general and to Harold's politics in particular, he couldn't help feeling a stir of interest in this lovely politician. She looked fresh and wholesome and had brown-flecked green eyes. Her cheekbones were high and softly etched, her nose was small and straight, and her mouth was molded with sensitivity. She was holding the soaked tissues out from her beige silk suit, and a smile tugged at the corner of Jake's mouth. *Pity the girl if Harold catches her in the act,* he thought. No sense of the ridiculous, Harold.

Crossing the parlor, Jacob called to her. "There's always the front door if you're leaving. That window's been stuck for years."

Whirling around, cheeks flushing pink, she stammered. "I—I wasn't leaving, I was just…"

"Attempting to litter," he finished for her, then laughed at the chagrin on her face. "Here, I'll take care of that for you."

She appeared reluctant to turn the mess over to him. "If you'll point me in the right direction, I'll take care of it myself. After all, it was *my* clumsiness."

"Harold startled you. I don't know what got into him, shouting like that. He's self-controlled ninety-nine percent of the time, not at all given to shouting. At least, not since we were boys playing board games."

With a confidential grin, he hoped to set her at ease. "He always accused me of cheating."

"And did you?"

"Only when I was losing. Here, give me that mess."

As he stepped out of the room, Natalie wondered if he would return, and she found herself, for no accountable reason, hoping he would. She hadn't long to wait, for he was already back.

"You're the fellow in the red TransAm, aren't you?" she asked as he settled beside her on the sofa.

"Yes, and you're the road hazard in the blue Pinto." He shot her a quick grin.

"Road hazard! I object."

His eyes were deep-set and blue, disturbingly blue as they danced in the humorous gaze that held hers. "I was all but seasick following you. You're the hare and the tortoise all rolled into one. And you scared a whole new set of wrinkles into Tex Meredith's face, swerving over in his lane like that."

Grasping the obvious, Nat asked, "You live here?"

"That I do, and I'm all ears, waiting to hear what brings you."

"I'm Natalie Franklin. Mrs. Brandon—your mother, perhaps?" She paused and was awarded a nod. "Mrs. Brandon ran an advertisement in *Gleanings*."

"Oh, the family history thing," he said, giving away neither pleasure nor displeasure.

"Yes. She's looking for a writer. I answered her ad and sent along some samples of stories and articles I've had published. After reading them, she arranged for this appointment."

"Only now Harold has trapped her in the library, and you're left waiting. I could break it up in there," he offered, a hint of mischief dancing in his eyes.

14

"Oh, no! That would be rude....What I mean is, I don't mind waiting. And I do want to make a good..." She stopped short. This babbling wasn't like her at all.

"Impression," he supplied the word. "I know; I've been there. All right, so we'll wait. And while we wait, I'll forewarn you—you haven't any idea what you're letting yourself in for."

"Why do you say that?"

"My mother has trunks overrun with old scrapbooks, diaries, faded newspaper clippings, county histories, and rambling memoirs of people who lived a hundred-odd years ago—dead history."

"But history is never truly dead. It touches the lives of those who follow. And the more information there is, the more interesting and accurate the account of Jacob Sutton will be."

"Interesting perhaps, but not necessarily accurate," he disagreed mildly. "In my opinion, there's been a good deal left out of those memoirs, not to mention some whitewashing of what was left in. And the diaries too often reveal nothing more than sentimentality."

"Then you're against the idea of a family history?" She experienced a sudden wave of defeat foreign to her optimistic nature.

A dark curl sprang onto his forehead as he shook his head. "No, I'm not against it. I simply think it's next to impossible to get an accurate view of Jacob Sutton from the available material. It's going to be difficult to sort fact from fiction. Do what you will with the warning."

"*If* I'm fortunate enough to be selected for the job."

"You're really counting on it then?"

"It's important to me, yes," she said.

"Why?"

She struggled to respond honestly to his blunt curiosity. "Because it's an opportunity to write," she said finally.

"And that's what you do best?"

He was laughing at her, not aloud, not even unkindly, but with that edge of experience an adult turns on a child. But she wasn't a child. She had a goal in mind and wanted this job to be a milestone along the way.

"Let's just say I write better than I drive and let it go at that." She refused to be provoked and was rewarded by his furtive reassessment. Having the edge now and determined to keep it, she turned the tables on him. "And what do *you* do best?"

"That all depends on whom you ask." He sidestepped her question and chuckled.

"Suppose I asked your mother. What would she say?"

"In the frame of mind I left her in three weeks ago, she would undoubtedly say I'm best at dodging what I don't want to do and doing as I please with a great show of virtue."

"And if I were to ask Hannah?"

"Hannah, is it?" He pretended to give it deep consideration. "Hannah would tell you I'm best at leaving socks turned wrong side out, a bed unmade, and candy wrappers close to but never quite in the wastepaper basket."

Clearly he was enjoying himself, weaving this mystery when all she really wanted to know was what he did for a living. Finding his manner mildly flirtatious,

Nat wondered if anyone had a claim on him. "And if I were to ask your wife?"

The change in him was so radical she instantly wished she could withdraw the question. He wrenched his gaze away from hers, studying the rug beneath his feet with a brooding expression.

"My wife is dead."

Hearing his voice, so flat yet fiercely controlled, she felt instant compassion. She had not meant to tear open an old wound with her thoughtless question. The intensity of the silence between them was a physical pain.

Softly, with a prayer in her heart, she murmured, "I'm sorry I stumbled into something so painful."

His smile was nearly as aching as his flash of anguish had been. "My fault," he said. "I led you right into it, playing cat-and-mouse with your questions. The thing is, we have a common interest."

"You're a writer?" She felt a glow of something shared.

"Of sorts," he said with modesty.

"You're being mysterious again," she chided. "What do you write, fiction or nonfiction?"

"Facts. I lack the imagination to embroider."

"Oh." It was hard to keep the disappointment from her voice, for fiction was her love. She could get lost in it, sometimes did. "But still, you're a writer. I haven't met many writers. Are you a newspaper reporter?"

"Close. Television. Or perhaps I should say I'm a used-to-be, not that far removed from a has-been." He offered a crooked smile, and she found herself doubting this man could ever be a "has-been."

"I was part of a foreign news team until a few years

ago. Now I do occasional documentaries for public broadcasting stations. And when time allows, I try my luck at free-lance articles for a variety of magazines—news journals, media magazines, occasionally a travel piece."

"See there! You really *are* a writer, and versatile, too. I imagine having traveled a lot helps, doesn't it?" She let out a small sigh of confession. "I'm a terrible homebody myself. A writer ought to be out experiencing places to write *about,* meeting interesting people and hearing new viewpoints. But I'm afflicted with this terrible illness."

"You are?"

"It's called homesickness," she confided in a whisper, and he laughed. "Really, I am. My mother scraped up the money to send me to church camp one summer. I was a big girl, too. Thirteen or fourteen at least. But after a day, I called home and cried so hard she sent one of my brothers to pick me up."

He laughed again, liking that she joined him in it, liking even more her confession.

"Where is home to you?" he heard himself ask.

"Lincoln. It's a small town midstate. Have you ever heard of it?"

"Sure. Named for the great emancipator." *How rich!* he thought. He wondered if this woman was sharp enough to scratch beneath the surface of Sutton family history to find the dark side of old Jacob Sutton. If Natalie did discover the truth, would she gloss it over? Or would she be a stickler for fact?

His mother, basically a truthful woman, had a streak of family pride and wanted to deny that darker side. Likewise with Harold—only his reasons were more self-serving. A United States senatorial candidate

18

wouldn't want the press to learn he had an ancestor accused of illegal slave-trading, catching runaways for a hefty reward, and worse—if anything could be any worse—catching blacks with freedom papers, destroying their documents, and selling them back into slavery.

If Jake wrote the book, there would be no glossing over. His mother wouldn't like it, but being his mother, she would forgive him, even respect his high regard for truth. Not so with Harold. Never! That was why Jacob had steadfastly refused to write the family history.

"Have I introduced myself? I'm Jacob Brandon. There has to be a Jacob every now and again in remembrance of old Jacob, you see. I've often wondered why Harold, the elder, wasn't given the dubious honor of the traditional name."

Natalie defended Mrs. Brandon's choice of names. "Jacob is biblical and chosen for a good reason. My name was just a hasty revision. After five boys, my parents had given up on a girl, and Mom went to the hospital armed only with boy names. When I surprised her, Nate became Natalie."

"A very nice name," he said, with admiring eyes. "Suits you much better than Nate."

For long stretches, talking to him seemed easy. Then suddenly he'd look at her in a certain way and she felt almost shy.

"Usually," she said, needing to fill a small silence, "it gets shortened to 'Nat.' "

A frown found its way between his thick brows. "I don't know—that sounds like a pesky drone in the ear. I think I'll stick with 'Natalie,' if you don't mind. And why don't you call me Jake?"

She wrinkled her nose, and he laughed. "What? Don't you like it?"

"It brings to mind images of a bowlegged prospector from some old Western," she said.

He laughed again, then said they didn't know one another well enough to make knowledgeable judgments on their nicknames. In a week or so "Nat" might come easily to him and "Jake" to her.

"You mean I could well become a pesky drone in your ear?" She was secretly pleased, if only because he said it as if her getting the job was a foregone conclusion. It had nothing to do with his dimpled smile melting her like sun-warmed milk chocolate.

"A bowlegged old prospector isn't too flattering, either," he pointed out.

They shared a smile, and Natalie was treated to another glimpse of dimples. But before she could make him smile again, the library door opened with a "whoosh" and Harold Brandon strode into the room.

Chapter Two

"All right, Mother. But when complications arise, I'll trust you to remember I did try to warn you," Harold shouted impatiently over his shoulder. He caught sight of Natalie just then, and dispelled the telltale signs of heated debate and frustration. He gave her a polite, impersonal smile.

She smiled back. He was a more compact, less vital version of Jacob. His hair was just as black but straight; his eyes were a more shallow blue. The same Roman nose was at the center of angular features, the chin was cleft but weaker, and the dimples were missing entirely. Harold looked past her to Jacob.

"Hello, Jake. I didn't know you were back. Mother wasn't expecting you for another week. And who is this charming lady you've brought along with you? A friend to meet Mother?"

He cocked a disparaging eyebrow at Jacob, and though Natalie discerned a sudden tension in the air, Jacob responded with an unruffled grin.

Natalie spoke first. "I'm Natalie Franklin. I've an interview scheduled with Mrs. Brandon for eleven."

Harold's mouth thinned out, and he blinked rapidly.

Had he been a magician, the blink would have reduced her to thin air. But he gave no verbal opposition to the interview. Rather, he extended a well-manicured hand and apologized.

"And here it is eleven-fifteen. I'm afraid Mother's kept you waiting, hasn't she? Allow me to show you in. Miss Franklin, you say? You must be the writer Mother's been telling me about."

The lukewarm hand that had gripped hers for a brief moment slid to her elbow as Harold Brandon propelled her toward the library.

Natalie glanced back to see Jacob's eyes harden. His mouth had lost all trace of good humor, and his dimples were in hiding. Now, why was he scowling?

The answer came in an intuitive flash. He had no patience with falseness. And if Harold was opposed to this family history, then his warm introduction to his mother, Marianne Sutton Brandon, was about as falsely welcoming as an introduction could be.

"Mother, this is Natalie Franklin. Miss Franklin, my mother, Marianne Sutton Brandon. I'm afraid we've kept Miss Franklin waiting, Mother. She tells me her appointment was for eleven."

Harold smiled graciously at Natalie as he urged her into a tapestry-cushioned chair facing a huge oak desk. As Mrs. Brandon apologized, Natalie silently surveyed her. She had eyes the same dynamic blue shade as her younger son's. There was a mixing of gray in her closely cropped and curled black hair, and a tasteful cosmetic application went far to conceal the fine lines fanning out from her mouth and eyes.

Nat also detected a regal poise as Mrs. Brandon lifted her head and said to her son, "If you'll excuse us,

Harold, Natalie and I will get on with the business at hand."

Harold's eyes sparked rebellion at the polite but firm dismissal, but he turned on his heel and paused in the doorway only long enough to mention, "By the way, Mother, Jake is home."

The spontaneous pleasure that leapt to the gracefully aging features left no doubt the news was welcome. In that moment, Mrs. Brandon seemed motherly, not at all the formidable aristocrat Nat had feared she might find.

"Would you mind too terribly if I delayed our interview just one moment longer, Natalie?" Mrs. Brandon asked, rising from behind the desk.

"No, of course not."

Flashing Natalie a grateful smile, Mrs. Brandon rounded the desk. She was a large woman, her bulk played down only slightly by a flowing caftan. Irresistibly drawn to the reunion in the parlor, Nat nudged her chair around to a view through the open door.

"Surprised you, didn't I?" Jake greeted his mother with a hug and a kiss. Their laughter ran together a moment while Harold stood to one side, his mouth stretched tight as a bowstring.

"So did you get all your dragons slain?" he asked Jacob with unmistakable sarcasm.

Keeping an arm around his mother, Jacob gave a casual reply. "A few here, a few there, but not the big granddaddy of them all. He didn't like my questions. In fact, he didn't like anything about me. So he cut our interview short and refused to give me a tour of his factory."

"How will we ever rest, not knowing if lethal fumes are leaking into the air from Rhaol-Tech?"

"Not necessarily lethal, Harold. No one has died yet. Just a high rate of absenteeism on the job, due to headaches, nausea…"

"Have you considered a flu bug?"

"It would have to be a very determined and powerful virus to keep sending so many employees home from work," Jacob said evenly, but even Natalie, who hardly knew him at all, recognized the clear spark of irritation in his eye.

Apparently Mrs. Brandon saw warning signs, too, for she interrupted. "You can tell us all about it at lunch, Jake. Harold, find Hannah, won't you, and tell her Jake's home. Perhaps she has some butterscotch pie left from dinner last night."

"The hero's welcome. Let's kill the fatted calf," Harold said.

Jacob appeared merely pained as one would be by a child's jealous outburst. But Mrs. Brandon's face suffused in color at her elder son's pettiness.

Acutely embarrassed for all three of them, Natalie swiveled to face the desk again.

Jake's voice sounded over Mrs. Brandon's footsteps. "Never mind, Harold. I'll find Hannah myself."

As Mrs. Brandon sank into the desk chair, a frown knit her brow and turned the edges of her mouth down.

Nat found herself wanting to pat the woman's hand and assure her that "boys will be boys." But, of course, it was more than that. They weren't boys. They were grown men.

With a concentrated force, Mrs. Brandon pushed aside whatever personal problems assailed her. She plunged into the interview, complimenting Natalie's writing style.

In turn, Natalie relaxed and confided she was an avid history fan and in recent weeks had boned up on southern Illinois history to get a feel for Jacob Sutton's era. She had also briefly researched the geography of the area and the method used to run the salt water through a crude pipework system of hollowed, mortared logs into large kettles where the water was boiled away until only salt crystals remained.

"It was for that era a very sound business wasn't it, Mrs. Brandon?"

The older woman assured her it was. "Salt was, of course, a staple to the pioneers. Frontier settlers came from great distances to buy it. Local farmers and tradesmen depended on the abundant supply of salt, too.

"The federal government kept the land surrounding the natural salt springs. Jacob merely leased the rights to the saltworks. The land he was able to purchase, the land this house sits on, in fact, is several miles north of the actual work sites."

"Considering the mode of transportation in those days, that must have been an inconvenience," Nat commented.

"I'm sure it was," Mrs. Brandon agreed. She went on to speak of the inexhaustible supply of salt and water and grass that made the valley a literal haven for wildlife, which in turn attracted explorers. She continued to share her knowledge until Hannah appeared to announce lunch.

"If the boys don't wish to wait, let them go ahead without me. I'll be another five or ten minutes," Mrs. Brandon told Hannah.

As Hannah gave a curt nod and left, Mrs. Brandon folded her hands on the desk and met Nat's gaze.

"You're young and inexperienced as a writer, Natalie. But I admire your forthrightness. I also like your work. It's lively. That is precisely what I want, a book to make the Suttons come alive.

"First and foremost, the book will be about Jacob. You will trace him from humble beginnings in Virginia through his migration to Illinois. And of course you will elaborate on his interest and success in working the salt springs.

"But Jacob was also a husband, a farmer, a pillar of the community, and, later, a politician. He greatly affected the lives of his children, nine of them boys, one a daughter. Some chapters will be devoted to the Sutton children—brief but enlivened biographies. Some of the descendants of these ten children became well-known, and I want you to mention them, too. The material I've gathered will help you."

Mrs. Brandon slid back from the desk to open a drawer and remove a skeleton key. "Before you make a final decision, I want to show you the room where I store material pertinent to the Sutton family history. Follow me, Natalie, and watch your step. The lighting is dim."

Mrs. Brandon unlocked a narrow door between some bookshelves, and Natalie followed her through the opening. A steep wooden staircase stood before them.

Mrs. Brandon began the ascent, her caftan billowing about her ankles. Natalie followed, reminded of a nineteenth-century romantic novel. *Back stairs for the servants,* she thought and hid a smile.

Perhaps it was a combination of weight and age that necessitated Mrs. Brandon's pause on the second-floor landing. Her voice winded, she said, "I don't come up here as often as I used to....I fear I'm out of shape."

While they waited, Natalie wondered about her odd feeling when Mrs. Brandon had put a key to the staircase door. It somehow clothed in mystery an ordinary climb up a narrow staircase.

Presently, Mrs. Brandon resumed the climb. Nat's heels rang hollowly on the steps to the third story. Here the landing ended in a T, a door to the right, a door to the left. Again Mrs. Brandon used the key, leading the way into what Natalie quickly realized was the tower.

The room wasn't well dusted, but there was an appealing simplicity in the brick walls and the pine floor untouched by paint or varnish. Natalie arched her head back, gazing up to where the ceiling peaked, half expecting to find an old cast-iron bell.

"It's a lovely view, isn't it?" Mrs. Brandon said, stepping up to one of the narrow windows set into each wall of the six-sided room. "A deer park is hidden there in the trees. And out the north window, you'll see the orchard in blossom. If we were to catch the wind from the right direction, we could even smell the apple blossoms through the open window."

Peacefully they stood side by side looking down on the restful scene. Plowed fields made gentle wavelets, flower gardens boasted a shower of color, and trees swayed like feather dusters in the breeze. "It's lovely," Nat murmured, almost regretful when Mrs. Brandon turned back to their purpose in visiting the tower room.

"These trunks are full of family memorabilia. You'll find old letters, scrapbooks, photo albums, diaries, newspaper clippings, and such. I'm sorry to say there isn't much order to them. It will be up to you, Natalie, to sift through it all and develop a sense of Jacob and his time.

"There are also reference books in the library downstairs. In fact, you might choose to work in the library. That's up to you. If you'd rather, I'll have a long table brought up here. Or you might even wish to use your bedroom."

It had not occurred to Natalie that she might be expected to stay at the house. But as she opened her mouth to question the arrangement, a male voice startled her into closing it again.

"Mother, you surely aren't going to put her to work without any lunch. Forgive her, Natalie. She's obsessed with this history thing." Jacob sauntered into the tower room, shaking his head in mock disapproval.

He flung an arm across his mother's rounded shoulders. "Soup's growing cold, and Hannah is fuming. Can't you finish this discussion after lunch?"

Coerced, Mrs. Brandon invited, "Would you stay for lunch, Natalie? Hannah can set another place."

Natalie politely demurred. She had no desire to discuss what remained of their business over lunch while Harold aimed gibes at Jacob and Jacob bore them with a humorless grin.

She was accustomed to a loving, loyal family and was loath to be drawn into undercurrents she did not understand. Mrs. Brandon did not press her to stay, for which Natalie was thankful. She was ready to be alone to sort out her thoughts.

As they descended the steps, Mrs. Brandon wound their discussion to a close. Natalie wondered briefly if the door across the third-story landing was locked, too—it probably led to one of those old-fashioned, half-finished half-story attics. "I'll be getting in touch with you by phone in a few days, Natalie. Once we work out the details, we'll sign a contract and you can consider yourself commissioned."

"I'll be looking forward to your call," Nat murmured as Mrs. Brandon locked the stairway door.

"I would like to make one point clear," Mrs. Brandon added, dropping the key into the desk drawer. "I don't want any of the family papers leaving this house. That's why I prefer you stay here at the house."

"If you're certain I won't be underfoot or make more work for Hannah."

"The house is large. We seldom stumble over one another. Jake is gone a good deal of the time. Harold is due to hit the campaign trail soon, which leaves only Hannah, Timothy, and me."

"Timothy?"

"Harold's son. He won't give you more than an occasional headache." Jacob gave Natalie a crooked smile.

"I have a horde of young nephews, so an occasional headache will be allowed in fair exchange for the pleasure of Timothy's company. How old is he?"

"Timothy is eight, and other than an occasional bout of mischief, he's a fine boy. As for Hannah," Mrs. Brandon continued, "she's a complexity. She staunchly refuses any outside help but isn't above grumbling over her workload. You'll soon learn simply to endure her cross side when it appears."

Mrs. Brandon looked as if she might elaborate, but Hannah peeked into the library at that moment. She approached Mrs. Brandon's desk. "You said lunch was to be served at noon, Marianne. Not knowing you'd changed your mind, that was the hour I aimed for."

29

"Forgive me, Hannah. I did say noon, and I haven't changed my mind, just fallen behind. Jacob, why don't you walk Natalie to her car?"

"Jake hasn't eaten either," Hannah objected, sliding Natalie a look which seemed to say, "See what a bother you are?"

Quickly, Natalie spoke up. "That's all right. I can find my own way out."

But Jacob was not the least intimidated by Hannah's scowl. "Just save me a piece of butterscotch pie, and I'll do without the soup and sandwich, Hannah."

"You'll do nothing of the sort. Lord only knows what kind of garbage you pack away while you're gone. Probably nothing but black coffee and butterscotch candy. You be in the dining room in five minutes, or the rest of us will eat without you, starting with the pie!"

"You old tyrant, you." He reached out and tweaked her pale cheek, then turned to take Natalie's arm. "Hurry along now. Hannah isn't one to make idle threats."

Natalie bade Mrs. Brandon a hasty good-bye and added, "It was nice meeting you, too, Hannah," before she allowed Jake to rush her out the way she'd come in.

She was relieved when he released her arm to swing open the front door, then followed her out without re-establishing a guiding touch. Though his hand on her arm had been polite, impersonal even, she'd found it unsettling.

"You're very subdued for a writer who just landed a job," Jake observed as he held open her car door. "I expected a more jubilant spirit."

"I guess I'm a little numb," she admitted. "I didn't

expect it to come that easily. The reaction will set in soon. Then I'll grin like an idiot all the way home."

The look he slanted her was shot through with understanding. "I know the feeling. We become so accustomed to scraping and wheedling and fighting for every opportunity, it's breath-stealing to get what we want without wearing ourselves out—or at least chewing our nails a bit."

Something was breath-stealing all right, though Nat wasn't at all sure it was the ease with which she'd landed the job. It had more to do with the man beside her, the pleasant surge of his voice. What was going on behind that dimpled smile, those cloudless blue eyes? Was he, too, feeling a shock of awareness?

She blushed at the bold thought. Of course he wasn't. He must be ten years her senior. He'd traveled the world as a foreign news correspondent, and he'd been married and suffered loss. Surely life no longer had any shock value for him.

Bashful over her unwarranted preoccupation, she slid behind the wheel of her blue Pinto. "You didn't seem at all surprised she gave me the job. Did you know ahead of time?"

"I was pretty certain, yes. You see, Mother has an odd quirk about this old house. She's very private about it, not given to inviting casual acquaintances in for tea, throwing lavish parties, or even asking aspiring young writers for interviews. So I concluded she'd already made her mind up about you before asking you here. Today's chat was a mere formality."

"You might have told me ahead of time. It would have made the waiting much easier."

She frowned then, thinking how proud she would be of the house if it were hers. "I'd think she'd love

31

showing off the house. It's beautiful. And considering her interest in history, it must be rich with stories."

A strange expression lit his face and was just as quickly dismissed. "I guess it's Mother's brand of privacy," he said. "In fact, for years she did all the housework herself to avoid granting care of the place to a housekeeper."

And now that she had a housekeeper, she locked certain doors. The oddity of that clung to Nat like fuzzballs to an old sweater. She knew Hannah had never cleaned the stairway or tower room. The dust and cobwebs would not have escaped her eagle eye.

"How did your mother come to find Hannah, then?" she asked.

"You know, with all your questions, you could be mistaken for a reporter," he noted with a smile.

"I'm sorry. I didn't mean to pry."

"Quite all right. Actually, you'd be a step ahead if you understood the situation. You see, Hannah is Harold's mother-in-law."

She felt her mouth form a round "O" and quickly shut it, closing in a barrage of new questions that sprang to mind. Where then, was Harold's wife? Mrs. Brandon hadn't listed her when she'd named off the residents. And why, if Hannah lived here as extended family, did she speak of Harold with such a tart sting.

Jacob continued his clipped explanation as if he were eager to have the explaining done. "Harold's wife, Jan, was Hannah's only child. When Jan was killed in the same plane crash as my wife's, Hannah showed up on our doorstep saying Timothy ought to have the attention of both his grandmothers. Mother'd been through a lot—all of us had—and in her emotional state, she hadn't the faintest idea how to cope with Hannah's determination to stay.

"Hannah made it clear from the start she wasn't a charity case, that she intended to earn her way. She has, too. Still, she isn't easy to understand. She loves Timothy and is good to him in her own firm, unyielding way. Yet she takes perverse pleasure in making Mother and Harold tread on eggshells. One moment she's as gentle and loyal as an old lap dog; the next she's on her high horse over muddy tracks in the foyer or leftovers missing from the refrigerator."

He fell silent then, his explanation as complete as he chose to make it. Not ready to voice any of the new questions in her mind, Natalie murmured, "Thanks for the warning. I'll wipe my feet without fail and keep my nose out of the refrigerator."

He rested his forearms on the open window, his gaze reflective and a bit hard to hold. "Don't let her intimidate you, Natalie," he said. "She has a bully's instinct. Get the limits settled in the beginning, and who knows? You might become the friend she so desperately needs."

There was a strange quality of caring about his warning—caring for a difficult old housekeeper and for a green writer, anxious to make good.

Recognizing that the caring quality about him drew her against her will and better judgment, Natalie said, "I'd better go so you don't miss your lunch."

He grinned and pulled a butterscotch candy from his pocket as she turned the ignition key. "I'm prepared for emergencies," he said, tossing a second candy into her lap.

Natalie accepted it with an upsweep of dark lashes. "She wasn't kidding about you, was she? You really do live on butterscotches."

"And black coffee. Don't forget the black coffee."

Chapter Three

Three weeks later Natalie returned to Sutton Valley. Spring was no longer a flirting tease but a promise fulfilled.

Tractors chugged across turned fields, and blooming clover filled the air with a heavenly fragrance. Farm wives glanced up from sprouting gardens to lift friendly hands as her blue Pinto sped by. Clotheslines sagged from heavy loads of laundry, and a family of ducks waddled across the road as if they had the perfect right to slow traffic.

Spotting the turnoff to the Brandons a short distance ahead, Nat slowed and touched her turn signal. Just as she leaned into the turn, a barefoot boy in bib overalls darted into the path of her car. She hit her horn and the brakes all in one motion. As he jumped back in alarm, the tip of his fishing pole whanged against her radio antenna.

The child stood frozen in his tracks, his freckles standing out on a face gone pale. Natalie saw by his expression he expected a scolding or at least a cross "Watch where you're going, kid!" But, she reasoned, as her heart slowed to a normal beat again, the scare itself had been scolding enough.

"Beautiful day, isn't it?" she called out her open window.

Relief brought the color back to his face by degrees. "Yes, ma'am." he murmured.

"You aren't playing hooky today, are you?" she teased.

"No, ma'am. I had a stomachache this morning, but it's better now."

Solemn though he was, he looked the picture of health. His glossy dark hair tumbled down on his forehead, his freckled cheeks were the warm shade of burnished copper, and his blue eyes were bright and alert. Nat could scarcely contain her laughter. Sick, indeed!

"Well, I'm glad you recovered. It's too nice a day to spend in bed."

"Yes, ma'am, it is," he agreed and with a boyish grin, he trudged on across the road.

Were he and the ducks headed for the same water hole? Nat hoped they were, for he looked the sort of boy who'd appreciate ducks. His polite "Yes, ma'am" was sweet and quaint from the lips of a child.

Natalie drove on, her heartbeat quickening as she made her way up the curving lane. This job she'd wanted so badly was hers. Praise God! She knew that in His master plan, there was woven a tiny thread—Nat Franklin's life. It touched other fine threads, other lives. Would it make a difference in the tapestry? It would—as long as she remembered her power source and didn't stray off on self-seeking tangents.

As they often did, Nat's thoughts and hopes and anxieties unconsciously blended into prayer. Prayer came as naturally to her as breathing and was accomplished with the same simplicity. Didn't God intend His love

36

to be so simple even a child could understand? Jesus set the example of that love, and she was to do the same. She was to love those whose lives touched hers.

As she stopped her car in front of the impressive old house, she thought fleetingly of Jacob's comment about Hannah. Hannah, no doubt, would be by far the most difficult to love with the love Christ intended.

Nat gave a small sigh. Putting love into practice when someone was anything but lovable was always a challenge. Yet weren't the unlovely the most starved for the caring of others? She would make it her goal to do just what Jacob had recommended. She would become a friend to Hannah.

Determined, Natalie tried not to mind moments later when a grim-lipped Hannah met her at the door.

"So you've come. Been a lot of commotion today— Timothy being home from school, Harold taking off, now you moving in. Leave your things here at the door. I'll take them up later." Hannah folded her arms as if she were hugging her disapproval tight.

Because her own arms were aching from the load, Natalie had no choice but to drop her luggage inside the door. She did not, however, intend to let Hannah lug her things up the stairs.

"Just let me rest my arms a moment. Then I'll take them up if you'll be kind enough to show me which room, Hannah."

Hannah neither accepted nor rejected her offer. With an impatient flick of her hand, she indicated Natalie was to follow her.

Noticing how the parlor gleamed with conscientious care, Natalie said, "Everything looks lovely, Hannah. It must keep you busy, looking after such a big old house."

"Yeah, and folks don't make it any easier, tracking in and out all day. 'Course I reckon we've seen the last of Harold for a spell. And Jake, on a good day, spends more time out than in."

"Jacob's still home then?"

Hannah paused, her knuckles poised to knock on the library door. She pivoted to face Natalie, her eyes narrowing.

"Yes, but just for the record, Missy, you aren't Jake's type. His wife was a redhead. Most beautiful woman you ever wanted to see. Kind of uppity to my way of thinking, though Jake never seemed to mind. Or maybe you didn't know he'd been married."

This old woman *was* going to be hard to warm up to. Viewing herself through Hannah's eyes for a split second, Natalie felt depressingly plain. Yet she bit back a hasty reply. "Yes, he mentioned it."

"Well, he hasn't had any woman friends that I know of since he lost Gina. So I wouldn't be getting my hopes up if I were you."

Natalie nearly choked on her indignation. "I think you misunderstand, Hannah. I didn't mean to imply a personal interest in Jacob."

Hannah snorted her disbelief. "Women been after that lad since he was knee-high to a grasshopper. My own girl, Jan, had quite a crush on him herself when she was young. 'Course, in the end, she chose Harold, him seeming to be more dignified and more liable to stay close to home, too. At least, it seemed that way at the time, but that was before he got so hot for politics."

Marianne Brandon chose that moment to sweep open the library door. With a smile that dropped years from her face, she welcomed Natalie to Sutton Valley

Estate and Hannah immediately left the room.

"I can't begin to tell you how excited I am about getting this project underway," Marianne said.

Natalie's return smile expressed equal anticipation. "I'm looking forward to it, too, Mrs. Brandon. In fact, I can't wait to get started."

"I wish you'd call me Marianne. We're on informal footing here. Of course you remember my son, Jake," she added, stepping to one side as she gestured for Nat to take one of the chairs facing the desk.

Because Marianne had been blocking Nat's vision, she had not until that moment realized they were not alone. Her pulse quickened as Jake rose from behind the desk and engulfed her small hand in a firm grip.

"Good to see you again, Natalie." Sincerity was in every cadence, and he stood regarding her with a sparkle of interest in his blue eyes.

Nat's mouth went suddenly dry. Discouraged that he should affect her so—especially after a dose of Hannah's bluntness—she tried for a degree of composure.

"I'm pleased to be here," she murmured, and instantly she berated herself for being unable to come up with anything less tedious.

Lean and strong and in charge of the moment he regarded her calmly until she felt as if he'd reached out and stroked the betraying warmth into her cheeks.

She turned her attention to Marianne. "I hope I haven't come at a bad time. Hannah mentioned Timothy was home and that Harold left today."

"Yes, he's started the campaign circuit. He's kept both Hannah and me hopping the last couple of days, helping him prepare for the trip. But the house should settle back to normal now. As for Timothy, I believe he was just a little upset over his father's leaving. Nothing major, or course, but enough to make his stomach hurt."

Jacob leaned against the desk with one hand thrust into the pocket of his gray trousers. "Why don't I clear out of here so you two can get down to business?"

"But it's so near lunch time now," Marianne said. "Perhaps it would be best if Natalie settled in first. We can have our talk later this afternoon, though the way I feel, I'll need a nap first. I fear old age is creeping up on me," she said with a little laugh.

Jacob wrapped an arm around his mother and gave her a hug. "Nonsense. You've just had a lot on your mind."

Marianne gave him an appreciative smile. "It's good of you to help with the farm ledgers, Jake. I know you find it dull."

"Harold's done his part, handling the business end of the farm without complaint all these years. It won't hurt me to take a turn at it. If Harold wins a senate seat, he won't have time for the farm."

Agreeing, Marianne suggested, "While we're waiting for lunch, why don't you show Natalie around, Jake? And you might check in on Timothy, too. If he's hungry, I'll fix a lunch tray for him."

Jacob did his mother's bidding and found Natalie good company. There was an openness about her that he liked, though her enthusiasm for the project before her gave him an uneasy twinge. He went out of his way to make it an informative tour, pointing out the few remaining pieces that had been in the house in old Jacob's day.

Hannah was busy in the kitchen and ordered them out before they were three steps in. Jacob chuckled.

Feeling it only fair to warn her, he confided to Nat as they climbed an open staircase, "Hannah's having a bad day. She thought Timothy should go to school, but Mother overruled her. It isn't something Mother does very often, but she thought Tim might be a little anxious over his father."

"Poor kid," Natalie murmured sympathetically.

He chuckled again. "Poor us, you mean. Hannah's been vicious all morning, and with Tim off safe in his bedroom, the rest of us have borne the brunt of her tongue."

"You seem to be bearing up rather well," she said with a laugh in her voice.

He acknowledged her observation with what he hoped was a modest shrug and swung open the door to the room that would be hers throughout her stay. He watched her reaction to the rosebud paper lining the walls, the lacy spread and canopy on the four-poster bed, and the frilly sheer curtains around the window. Her footsteps muted in the thick, rose-hued carpet, she crossed to check out the view.

"Homesick already?" Jake asked, as she gazed off to the north.

Coloring prettily, she voiced misgivings. "Perhaps I shouldn't have made that confession."

"Be glad you did. Now we'll understand if you get misty-eyed over letters and phone calls from home."

She laughed as she tested the sheer fabric of the curtains, letting it glide through her fingers. "If I'm reduced to tears of homesickness, I'll simply drive home for a visit. I'm no longer thirteen and at the mercy of camp counselors."

"Worse, you're at the mercy of Mother. She's zealous about this book. And then there's Hannah to

41

contend with." He realized his words sounded like a last-ditch effort to make her reconsider her decision to write the book, but apparently she didn't think so, for she replied with soft conviction.

"Hannah and I are going to be friends. I've made up my mind about that."

"Good for you," he said in surprise.

The approval in his voice was as soothing to her as honey to a sore throat. She turned her attention out the window again. "It's a spectacular view."

His arm brushed hers as he stepped up beside her to point out the orchard beyond the green backyard. Farther in the distance a clover field made a circular path to the peak of a hill. But the timber that housed a deer park, interested her most.

Jacob stirred beside her. Though she could feel his gaze on her, she was slow to draw her eyes from the window. His scrutiny made her uncomfortably aware of him as a man.

Summoning her courage, she sent him a furtive glance. He held her to it, as if he'd been waiting, wanting her undivided attention.

"I've been looking forward to your coming, Natalie."

The directness of his words took her by surprise. "You have? But why?"

"I don't know…maybe because you're certain to bring matters to a head that have been concealed for a long time. When I figure out why, you'll be the first to know."

She moved away from him, fiercely insisting to herself she didn't feel deflated, hadn't wished for more personal words. She *was* feeling alarm, and why not? She had no wish to be caught up in the undercurrents and conflicts between Marianne's two sons. And the relationship between Marianne and Hannah seemed anything but smooth.

She jumped when Jacob came up behind her and placed a hand on her shoulder to turn her to him. With a hint of restrained laughter, he asked, "What? Regrets already?"

"No. I've wanted this job as badly as I've ever wanted anything."

"But?"

"I guess I'm a little tired. The long drive down must have caught up with me. I was all bubbly and excited this morning, believe me."

"I do." Without warning, he leaned down and kissed her. Not much of a kiss, perhaps, just a lightning-swift brushing of lips. But it was enough to throw her world off balance, to make her forget for an instant her resolve to keep a firm grip on her heart, to protect her dreams of becoming a truly great writer from the crippling distraction of a man's love.

But that was crazy! It was a simple, meaningless kiss. She felt instantly disloyal to her dreams and spoke with more fervor than she'd intended. "I wish you hadn't done that."

For the first time since she'd met him, he looked a bit uncertain. "Really? Perhaps I shouldn't have, then. I tend to act first and think later, a practice which has gotten me into a good deal of trouble over the years. Should I apologize?"

"No, that isn't necessary."

"Just don't let it happen again, eh?" He no longer looked uncertain; rather he appeared amused, as a man of experience might be by a prim and proper woman of far less experience.

She flushed hot and ducked her head to hide it. "Look, let's just forget it, okay?" He was quiet for so long she was compelled to sneak a look at him. Laugh lines bracketed his mouth.

"I'm not sure I can, now that you've made such a big deal of it. Big deals tend to stick in my mind, and sometimes they grow even bigger until I find myself wondering if I can perfect whatever I did that I wasn't supposed to do. Do you suppose I could?"

If Hannah thought he had lost an interest in women, she had her head buried in a sand trap! Refusing to dignify his teasing with a response, Natalie acted as if she'd dismissed the entire conversation.

"I guess I might as well do some unpacking before lunch."

"I'll get your luggage for you," he offered. "You're looking a little tired from the long drive down. Rest a minute, why don't you?"

"But I've some things in my car to unload, too."

"They'll wait. Sit down there and take a breather." He gave her a guiding hand to the desk chair, then went after her luggage.

Perhaps it was Hannah's offhanded reminder she was a plain woman not at all likely to attract the attention of such a man as Jacob that drew Natalie toward the mirror. Postponing the moment of truth, she put her nose into a bouquet of lilacs on the dresser. But only for a second, for she'd long since given up lamenting her ordinary appearance.

Her figure was slim but average, her brown hair fell below her shoulders and her eyes were green. When she smiled, which was often, her face did light up with a special warmth, or so she'd been told. But then everyone looked better when he smiled.

44

No, she would never be wolf-whistle material. Whatever attention she garnered from Jacob could only be due to kindness...or boredom.

Her response to his kiss was upsetting. She'd neither shied away nor flared with resentment. The plain truth was she'd liked being kissed by him. His lips had touched hers to a golden glow, and the glow had spread till her whole body tingled with its warmth. And then she'd overreacted, making a "big deal" of it by blurting out half-hearted objections.

She ran her fingers through tangled hair—she did look tired—and released a trembly sigh. Hannah now seemed a fraction of a problem compared to Jake's kiss.

Suddenly he was Jake. Now how had he become so familiar all at once? How indeed? He simply had, that was all. How an innocent kiss could change things! She was up to her knees in an emotional tangle. She had no wish to care for him in that special way, just when her writing career was getting off the ground. No, she could not succumb to this sudden weakness for blue eyes, deep dimples, a dark mustache, and curly black hair. She'd forget all about that kiss!

"I'll drop these here, but you'll have to wait to do your unpacking. Lunch is ready."

Nat whirled around to find him back with her suitcases. With a lurch of her heart, she knew if she ever did forget his kiss, it would be far off in the future. Well, pretending she'd dismissed it would have to do. For she didn't dare give away that he could steal her breath away with one look, a chance touch, the deep intonation of her name.

What had ever made her so brassily sure she was immune to masculine allure, she wondered as he stepped

45

to one side of the doorway to let her pass and the heady scent of his after-shave teased her senses.

He pointed her to the bathroom at the end of the hall. "Freshen up if you like, but don't take your time. Hannah's a bear about serving meals. Meanwhile, I'll check in on Timothy and see if he's interested in having lunch brought up."

She nodded agreement, though she was sure Jake wasn't going to find Timothy in need of a lunch tray. If her hunch was correct, he wouldn't find Timothy until he strolled down to the boy's favorite fishing hole.

But Jake didn't mention it. He ushered her down the stairs and into the dining room, all the while making polite chitchat, none of which involved Timothy.

Marianne and Hannah were both waiting for them in the dining room. After seating Natalie, beside Hannah and across from Marianne, Jake took the chair at the head of the table.

"Do I need to run a tray up to Timothy?" Marianne asked.

"No, that won't be necessary," Jake said.

Marianne appeared to be about to pursue the issue, but Jake forestalled her by bowing his head to offer thanks. His offering thanks not only surprised Natalie, it also touched her in some small way.

A delicious spinach salad, tossed up with young radishes and spring onions and creamy French dressing, was followed by club sandwiches cut into tidy triangles. Nat found she was quite hungry and lost no time praising the cook.

Hannah took it with an offhanded, "Isn't much to a salad and sandwich."

"But fresh green things taste so good," Marianne chimed in, wishing in her own dignified way to iron out the trouble spots of the day.

"With all she does, Hannah still finds time to tend a garden." Jake joined in on the crusade to soften Hannah's grim face.

Though Hannah didn't smile, warm pink spots did touch her cheeks. But too soon her pacified spirits were roused by a new discovery.

"Maybe I should take a tray up to Timothy," Marianne suggested, "even if he doesn't want it. Just a cup of soup perhaps. That should settle on his upset stomach."

"Don't go to the trouble, Mother. Tim isn't in his room," Jake said. He scooped into his pudding.

Hannah's thin hands clutched the edge of the table as she scooted her chair back. "He's run off, hasn't he? Marianne, I told you that boy wasn't sick. You're too soft on him, and that's a fact!"

"Now Hannah, I'm sure his stomach did hurt this morning. Every time his father leaves, he gets upset."

"Of course he gets upset! He learned early it's risky when folks leave. Sometimes they don't come back. But that's no reason to mollycoddle him. He's got to face up to his fear, not hide away." Hannah spat the words.

The appetizing lunch suddenly lost its appeal. The tension in the room made Natalie so uneasy she wanted nothing more than to get away. Not daring to look at Jake to see his reaction to Hannah's harsh words, Nat clutched her napkin tighter in her fist and tried to force down a bite of creamy butterscotch pudding.

When Jake spoke, his words came easily enough, so easily Nat was almost fooled into thinking Hannah hadn't made him think of his wife and how she, too,

47

had been lost to tragedy. "Personally, I think you're both making too much of it. An upset stomach isn't abnormal for a boy who's aware of reality. I think he handles himself quite well under the circumstances. Could even be he's taking a small advantage of the circumstances."

"What do you mean, Jacob?" Marianne asked.

Jake grinned. "Don't tell me you've forgotten how it is with little boys when the air gets sweet and warm and the school year's nearly ended. Classrooms become unbearably stuffy, and all the things that capture a child's imagination are on the other side of the window."

"You mean he told us his stomach hurt so he could skip school?" The idea obviously hadn't once occurred to Marianne. Jake laughed and shook his head, but there was no laughter on Hannah's face. Her eyes snapped and her mouth was a thin line of harsh disapproval.

"Take it easy, Hannah. I'll find him and try to point out the error of his ways—if I can remember exactly what the error is when I get there," Jake offered, his eyes twinkling with mischief.

Hannah continued to grumble under her breath about the folly of spoiling a child rotten. In faint hope of patching up the disturbance, Natalie let a moment or two pass before expressing her appreciation for her room. She made a special point of adding her thanks for the bouquet of lilacs, suspecting Hannah had put them there. From Hannah's gruff, "Lilacs aren't any trouble," she knew she'd guessed correctly.

Funny... woman so harsh on the outside possessing a fondness for gardening and flowers. One who worked close to nature couldn't help being caressed by the hand of God.

As they finished dessert, Marianne said, "I'm glad you're pleased with the room, Natalie. It's one of my favorites, too. I guess I mentioned you're welcome to work up there. The desk is old but quite serviceable.

"But you're free to use the tower room also. It's odd, but sometimes when I'm in the tower I feel rather close to the people who've lived in this house. When I look out over the land I know it must have looked much the same in old Jacob's day."

Having launched a subject less controversial than correct childrearing, Marianne stayed with it until the meal ended. Then she excused herself from the table to sneak in a short nap.

Though Natalie offered to help Hannah clear the table, Hannah wouldn't hear of it and actually seemed insulted by the offer.

"Why don't you go with me to find Timothy?" Jake suggested kindly to ease Nat's embarrassment. "Mother's 'short naps' sometimes stretch out half the afternoon."

She wanted badly to go. A dangerous confession for a woman who was determined to hold her emotions in check. "I should unpack my suitcases and unload the car," she offered lamely.

But Jake wasn't taking "no" for an answer. "All that will wait. Or hadn't you heard Rome wasn't built in a day? Come along, Natalie. It's a beautiful day."

The carrot he dangled was simply too tempting—a welcome walk away from this house and the gloom of Hannah's ugly moods.

His guiding hand fell away from the small of her back as they stepped out onto the veranda. At the bottom of the steps, he paused a moment, dragging in a deep breath, and shot her a crooked grin. "Hannah can cast a spell when she puts her mind to it, can't she? I feel I should apologize."

Uncomfortably aware he was anxious over her reaction to the lunch-table squabble, Nat murmured, "All families have their moments, I guess."

"Sweet though you are, you don't have to pretend you weren't shocked. Those green eyes of yours got very round and large."

Feeling warm despite the breeze stirring her cap-sleeved yellow dress, she took a more honest stand. "She is a bit much, isn't she?"

Jake threw back his head and laughed. "There, that's more like it. Don't ever be afraid to be honest with me, Natalie. I find honesty a very precious commodity and far too hard to come by. And yes, she is, to say the least."

"But if it helps any, confrontations between Mother and Hannah don't happen very often. It's just that Hannah was upset over Harold's leaving, too, but too blamed crusty to admit it."

He shoved his hands into his pockets. As they strolled down the lane, Nat was sure he knew exactly where to find Timothy. Had Timothy pulled this stunt before? Or had Jake, as a boy, done his own school skipping? She found it hard to think of him as a small boy. He was so much a man, tough flesh, muscles, and a mustache that had tickled when he kissed her. Soft velvet wings fluttered in her stomach, and she fiercely stamped out the memory.

"I wouldn't have guessed from her behavior she thinks that highly of Harold."

Aware she was subtlely prodding for more information, he eased out a weary sigh. "She's hard to understand, all right. I don't think she wants to care for Harold or for anyone, except Timothy. I'm not sure if losing her only daughter turned her that way or if she's always been afraid of loving."

"Then you didn't know Hannah until after her daughter died?"

Already the way was growing slippery, yet he answered, choosing his words carefully.

"No, not really, except as the mother of a schoolmate—Jan and I were in the same class. She always seemed a little grim to me. But she doted on Jan. Maybe she thinks it was wrong of her to be devoted to her only child. That would explain her taking a different approach with Timothy."

"It's all rather sad, isn't it?" Nat said after a moment.

He looked at her sharply. "Being afraid to love? Yes, indeed, it's sad. Foolish, too. To my way of thinking, love is God's greatest gift."

With a leaden spirit he thought of Gina, of their love. How bright a flame it had been but how quickly it had burned. Like a gas log in a fireplace, it had gone out all at once. It had been a tinsel thing, an illusion, and after all this time he still felt a deep sense of regret and shame.

He glanced down at the woman beside him, attracted as always by her freshness and her trusting nature. He couldn't tell her about Gina, not yet. Perhaps never.

Reaching the end of the lane, he stopped to face her and turned her chin up to look into her green and gold eyes. "You know, Natalie," he began, "just for the record, I appreciated your words of kindness to Hannah. She takes fresh flowers to Jan's grave a couple of times a week and decorates the house with them. Don't be discouraged by Hannah's rebuffs. It's just her way."

He seemed to expect an answer, a reassurance that she understood that fruits of kindness took time. In that moment, she felt very close to him, as if they shared similar viewpoints, similar ideals, similar values. Just for that short space in time, she treasured the closeness and felt neither surprise nor a need to draw away when he enfolded her small hand in his large warm one. It was his way of thanking her for troubling herself over Hannah. And she accepted the gesture as such, nothing more.

Or so she told herself, anyway.

Chapter Four

Natalie soon settled into the Brandon household, adjusting to each person in the family and to a steady work schedule. Because she was being paid a generous sum to do the Sutton history, she gave most of her day to it.

Slipping out of bed before daylight, she devoted a few moments to Bible reading and prayer, getting each day off to a peaceful and purposeful start. By the time dawn stretched fiery fingers across the sky, she was dressed and at her typewriter, plotting out in rough draft her historical saga. By breakfast time, she'd accomplished three to six pages.

After breakfast each day, she climbed the narrow wooden staircase to the tower room. There she immersed herself in Sutton family history. In a few weeks she had amassed a mountain of note cards and developed an emotional feel for the first Jacob Sutton and his descendants.

One day followed another until the rising temperature warned that spring was fast making way for summer. Marianne suggested Natalie might be more comfortable doing her researching and note taking in the air-conditioned library rather than the tower room, which was unshaded and oppressively warm by midday.

Natalie declined, however. Jake, who had become increasingly disturbing in his friendly fashion, spent a good bit of time in the library, working on farm ledgers and magazine articles. He would be a hopeless distraction.

Anyway, she was drawn to the tower room for reasons she did not entirely understand.

Like Marianne she felt closer there to Jacob Sutton and his descendants. Could she ever accurately recapture the personalities of those individuals—their pain, their joy, their best-kept secrets?

She was so intrigued with the challenge she often descended the steps with marked regret when dinner was announced. With the family gathered around the table, she had to put aside the historical puzzles and deal with the twentieth-century occupants of the old Sutton home.

Marianne was never a problem. Always warm and hospitable, she showed enthusiastic interest in the progress of Natalie's work.

Timothy, too, was a joy. Appreciative of the fact she never tattled on him for running in front of her car, Timothy was a steadfast friend. After school each day, he filled her ears with little-boy chatter of baseball card collections and who was the fastest runner at school. After dinner they sometimes played a docile game of naming shapes in the clouds as they lounged on a green hillside. Sometimes it was a session of baseball, sometimes a worm hunt for an upcoming fishing stint. More often than not, Jake joined in the fun.

Only when Harold was home were the evenings

more subdued. Though Timothy loved his father, he showed it with an awed respect. Natalie found it a sharp contrast to the warm love he showed all the others around him, including his grandma Hannah, who got a tight hug and a kiss each night.

When Harold was gone, Nat all but forgot he existed. But when he came home unexpectedly, as he did one weekend late in May, he brought strain with him. It settled over the house like an invisible cloak.

Not that the household was ever free of tension— Hannah saw to that. Some days she was sharply critical, others she remained aloof, and once she'd astounded Natalie by bringing a fresh-baked sweet roll and a glass of cold milk to her in the tower room.

Harold, at least, was consistent. He never missed an opportunity for a dig at Jake. On Saturday evening at dinner the dig came indirectly. "Timothy, haven't you forgotten something?" Harold was holding the chair for his mother.

Poor Timothy flushed and clambered out of his chair to seat his grandmother Hannah, who accepted it with little grace. She found Harold's harping on manners pretentious.

Jake, who was already seated, grinned and excused himself for not gallantly seating Natalie. "These modern women—you can't be too careful, Tim. They might take offense at the gesture, think you didn't credit them with the intelligence to seat themselves."

At Jake's broad wink in Natalie's direction, Harold responded with a cool, "I'll thank you not to undermine my authority, Jacob. Timothy will be well-bred despite opposing influence."

Meaning Jake. Natalie bristled. Jake was a model

gentleman in all the ways that counted—kindness, sensitivity, compassion.

She cleared her throat and filled the heavy silence. "Let's make a deal, Jake. You seat me on Monday, Wednesday, and Friday. I'll seat you on Tuesday, Thursday, and Saturday, and on Sunday we'll both seat ourselves."

Jake laughed and agreed, but Nat, embarrassed by her outburst—it had come out too loud, too defensive, and too contentious—missed his warm, blue-eyed look of gratitude.

The meal progressed from bad to worse. Harold criticized Timothy for putting his elbow on the table, for talking with his mouth full, and finally for dashing away from the table without being excused.

Belatedly, Timothy mouthed the necessary words. "May I be excused from the table, sir?"

Natalie thought she'd burst with irritation, a feeling which seemed to be shared by Hannah, who muttered under her breath, "What a great muck about nothing."

But Harold ignored his mother-in-law's interference and answered serenely. "Yes, you may, Timothy. And that's much better."

Timothy paused in the doorway between dining room and kitchen. "Are you coming out to play pitch and catch with me, Natalie?"

"I'll be right out, okay?"

He responded with a sweet grin. "Great! I'll get my ball and glove and meet you out front, Nat." He would have raced off, but Harold stopped him in his tracks with a stern, "Timothy! You've forgotten all the manners it took me eight years to drill into you. Miss Franklin is your elder. You must treat her with respect. From now on, you are to call her Miss Franklin."

56

It was more than Natalie could take. She tossed her napkin on the table. "Oh, for Pete's sake! I'm twenty-four, not eighty-four. No one calls me Miss Franklin, no one but you, Harold, and I'd thank you to stop it!"

"As you wish. Natalie, then," Harold said with no show of emotion. "However, this is an exception."

"Give him some credit! I'm sure he understands that," Natalie burst out and earned a swift kick under the table and a warning look from Jake. Feeling betrayed, she turned her scowl on him. One corner of his mouth twitched at her look of outrage. Then he shrugged as if to say *Okay, it's your funeral.*

Natalie instantly backed down. "Forgive me, Harold. That was rude. I can understand your concern that Timothy be well-mannered. But he is, after all, a very bright boy. I'm sure he understands it's because he and I are good friends that formalities are unnecessary."

The atmosphere was stiff with silence. Timothy slipped away unnoticed. Hannah's eyes showed a glimmer of admiration and slid from Natalie to the untouched meal she'd prepared. Marianne looked from her elder son to Natalie, then quickly away. Only Jake seemed relatively calm but with a catlike watchfulness.

"Your apology is accepted, Natalie, and your point well made," Harold said. "Timothy is a bright boy. I worry, though, when I'm gone so much, that he will begin to imitate a role model that is not altogether acceptable."

"Meaning me, I suppose." Jake pushed his chair back from the table.

Marianne blanched. "Jake, I'm certain he didn't mean you. You've a wonderful way with Timothy."

"Which is precisely what worries me." Harold made

himself perfectly clear as he rose to his feet to face his brother. "Do you know what I think? I think it bothers you that you don't have a son of your own. You'd like to influence Timothy more than an uncle has a right to."

A muscle along Jake's clean jawline grew taut. Harold had in some way scored a hit. Hurt for the unvoiced emotion that darkened Jake's eyes, Natalie scarcely heard Marianne's frazzled, "Stop it, Harold. That's enough."

"More'n enough, I'd say," Hannah muttered. She sniffed and looked at Natalie. "Why don't we clear the table now? Why I bothered cooking all this is beyond me."

Thrown off guard for only a minute, Nat seized the opportunity for action. Anything was easier than watching Jake cover the stark emotion Harold had deliberately triggered.

Once in the kitchen with Hannah, it was a relief to listen to the housekeeper's fretting over the sin of wastefulness as she stashed dishes of leftovers in the refrigerator. As Hannah droned on, Natalie ceased to catch her words, hearing only the flow of her voice, her inflection.

Nat was absorbed in trying to define the red-hot anger Harold had stirred in her. She didn't even entirely understand Jake's look of pain, and still she wanted to strike out in his defense. Harold had attacked coldly, deliberately, knowing Jake's weakness and taking advantage.

There! That was it! In her daily association with him, Jake seemed bright, witty, fun and caring—all man in the best of ways. She had seen no weakness in him. None.

But now Harold had pointed out that Jake, like every mortal, had weaknesses. And she didn't want to know that, didn't want to admit his weaknesses might well be tied up with a wife he had loved and who could not be replaced. Had Gina been unable to bear children?

"It's clean, child. The flower doesn't come off." Hannah spoke with uncustomary gentleness as she took the dinner plate from Natalie's hands and rinsed it in the other side of the double sink.

"What made Harold do that, Hannah?"

A mask of caution stole the softness from Hannah's face. "There's some things you'll never understand about these folks, Natalie. Best just leave it be. Jake's a big boy. He can take care of himself."

"But Harold was cruel to him. I don't really understand why, but I know he was. They're brothers!"

"Best stay out of it, Missy. Anyway, didn't I warn you not to set your hopes on Jake?"

Were her feelings for Jake really that visible? Nat set to work on the silverware scattered in the sink. She'd been so sure she had her emotions well in hand, had kept her relationship with Jake on a light, friendly plane. She talked with him over meals, included him in her play with Timothy, took occasional sunset walks with him, sometimes linking hands, sometimes not.

She'd tried not to make too much of his handholding. Jake was one of those people to whom touching just seemed to come naturally. He was forever tossing Tim into the air, ruffling his hair, clapping him on the back. He was affectionate with his mother and occasionally even embarrassed Hannah with a hug.

As if thinking of him produced him in person, Jake strolled into the kitchen, and with a plucky grin he untied Hannah's apron strings.

"Hannah, you old dear," he wheedled, "do you have any of those butterscotch cookies stashed away?"

"You and your butterscotch," Hannah growled. "It's a wonder you don't turn into a butterscotch."

A finger to his mustache, Jake struck a thoughtful pose. "And what exactly *is* a butterscotch? Would you grow one in the ground? Or on a tree, perhaps? Would you know one if you saw one, Hannah?"

Hannah had a low tolerance for nonsense. "Blamed if I know. The cookies are on the bottom shelf of the cupboard there. Help yourself. Then get out of my kitchen—it's crowded in here."

"Timothy's warming up out there. He's going to be a crack pitcher one of these days," Jake said as he helped himself to a handful of cookies. Then with a tweak of Hannah's cheek and a wink in Nat's direction, he sidled out of the kitchen.

After a moment, Hannah briskly ordered Nat out, too. "You run along now; the boy is waiting." Nat was at the front door before she stopped to wonder which boy? Jake or Timothy? Hannah had a weakness for both, though if accused she would have hotly denied she kept stocked up on butterscotch sweets simply because Jake had a liking for them.

Marianne stood at a window, its curtain drawn aside. With a twinge of guilt Nat recognized the strain drawing her mouth down. She joined the woman for a moment, and together they watched Jake and Timothy throw a baseball back and forth. Harold was nowhere to be seen.

Nat drew a steadying breath. "Marianne, I'm sorry I spoke out of turn at dinner. I feel responsible for the unpleasantness."

Marianne held back quick tears of surprise. She

reached for Natalie's hand and gave it a squeeze. "Don't apologize, Natalie. It had nothing to do with you. This trouble between Harold and Jake isn't recent. I keep praying they will someday, someway, be friends again. But maybe that prayer won't be answered in my lifetime. Who can say?

"They've seen you, Natalie. You'd better run on out before Timothy breaks out in hives from the wait. Such an impatient lad!" She clucked, but her voice was soft with affection.

Nat hadn't taken time to change out of her blue lace and eyelet sundress, so it would have to be a tame baseball game. She ran out to join them. In her enthusiasm, she forgot her resolution before long. Timothy wanted to bat, Jake agreed to field his hits, and Nat pitched straight across the plate. She would have made her brothers proud.

Timothy soon took a turn at pitching with Nat fielding and Jake batting. Wherever she stood, Jake hit the ball farther than she anticipated, and in a short while, she was breathless from the workout. Uncomfortably warm, panting, she pleaded, "Let's call it quits, okay, Tim?"

"Ah, Nat!" He jutted out his lower lip and prepared to argue for a few more minutes of play, but Jake forestalled him. "I'm all in, too, Tim. We'll play another time, though it seems to me you're in pretty good shape for little league. Think you'll hit any home runs this season?" he asked, draping an arm across Tim's shoulder.

"I think I might have a chance at it," Tim said, accepting the bat from Jake and the fielder's glove from Natalie.

Now why couldn't Harold be a friend to the boy as

well as a father, Nat wondered. There was pleasure behind the boy's cautious modesty, pleasure in Jake's noticing his progress, pleasure in Jake's praise. What a pity Jake didn't have children of his own.

Jake shrugged tired shoulder muscles, the black knit of his shirt expanding across his broad chest. He grimaced and complained. "You know, Tim, you've been giving us quite a workout."

Tim said, "You keep up pretty good for an old guy, Uncle Jake." Nat could not hold back her laughter.

Jake arched a brow of mock offense and said, as he swiped a bronzed hand across a damp, curl-strewn forehead, "You think that's funny, do you?"

Sometimes, even in play, Nat's suppressed feelings rose dangerously close to the surface. Her heart seemed to swell and pulse as he closed the distance between them, twin sparkles dancing in his eyes.

Hastily, she backed off. "Old? Who said you were old? I agree with the adage, 'You're as young as you feel.' "

Fairly oozing vitality, he latched onto her wrist with one strong hand, Tim's with the other, and boasted, "At the moment, I feel young enough to wrestle you both to the ground and make you say 'Uncle.' "

"Uncle," Natalie said, before he could make good his threat. She kicked off her sandals, folded her feet beneath her, and sat as serene as Miss Muffet on her throne.

"Some challenge that was," Jake said.

"You forget, I have brothers. The time to cry 'Uncle' is before the fight ever starts."

A suggestive quality hidden beneath his laughter brought color to her cheeks. She busied her hands, first repositioning the lawn sprinkler next to her, then gathering a handful of tousled hair off her neck. The soft breeze air-dried her neck and cooled her cheeks.

Her composure restored, she glanced up at him and said, "Anyway, it's too hot for such nonsense. All I'm interested in is a shower, and even that will have to wait. I'm too lazy to move."

"You know, she's right, Tim. It's time you were heading for the showers, too. Don't you have some homework to do?"

Timothy groaned. Jake released his wrist to tug at his ear lobe. "You'd better go in now, don't you think?"

Tim took off at a dead run, yelling back, "Okay, Uncle Jake, but you'll have to catch me first!"

Nat had a front-row seat for the entertainment. Tim led Jake on a giggling, weaving chase all over the front lawn. Jake ran effortlessly, calling out threats, yet letting the boy keep a lead of a few feet.

Nat cheered Tim on, calling out encouragement. "Keep running, Tim! He's losing ground. You're too fast for him—his tongue's hanging out. Keep running!"

The pair of them disappeared around the side of the house, made a full circle and were back again. Tim's face was red and glistening with sweat, and his legs were slowing like a wind-up toy winding down. He cast a glance back over his shoulder and, still laughing, tripped over the garden hose.

As he fell to the ground in a panting heap, Jake was upon him. Seeing the boy was unhurt, he tickled him a second, then pulled him to his feet. "Now off to the showers, then homework before Grandma Hannah starts scolding."

Before Tim could obey, Jake leaned to whisper in his ear. Tim nodded, then gathered up the baseball equipment and headed toward the house. Nat saw him shoot a questioning glance back over his shoulder, but couldn't give it proper thought. She was too busy with the swirl of feelings Jake's nearness triggered.

Planting his hands on his lean hips, Jake gave her his full-fledged attention. "As for you, Miss Nattie, sweet drone in my ear, I'll have you know my tongue was *not* hanging out of my mouth. I may not have won any track trophies lately, but I can still catch an eight-year-old boy. So are you going to apologize for the insult or take the consequences?"

She accepted his hand up and grinned back at him. Even if he wasn't breathing hard, his pulse was beating out a fast tap dance. But then, so was hers. Her heart tumbled against her rib cage as he caught a handful of hair and tickled her cheek with the silky strands.

She tried to meet the blue warmth of his eyes, but halfway there she faltered and settled instead on a loose thread in the second buttonhole of his shirt. An idle finger whisked it away.

He made a mustache over her lip with a strand of her own hair and demanded, "Are you going to apologize or not?"

She caught a ragged breath and on an upsweep of lashes saw nothing but boyish laughter on his features. His handsome face was relaxed, his stance was easy, his eyes were bright with merriment. Shamed that he could so effortlessly disturb her and at the same time be so calm she quipped, "No apology and no consequences. I'm off to the showers!"

As she stepped away from him, he ripped the air

64

with a rich laugh. "How right you are! Any time now, Tim!" he shouted, and he sprinted halfway across the yard.

Bewildered by the anticipation on his face as he turned to look back at her, she bent down to pick up her sandals. As rotten luck would have it, she was standing right over the lawn sprinkler when it leaped to life with a spray of cold water. Jake's laughter was louder than her shocked yelp.

Clutching her sandals, she dashed out of reach of the sprinkler. But the damage was done. Her dress hung like a limp rag, her hair was plastered to her head, and tiny rivulets of water dripped off her nose and chin.

"You...you...you rat!" she shouted. She tossed first one sandal, then the other, at Jake, who was still shaking with laughter.

Tim peeked around the corner of the house, his sheepish grin turning to something more worried as he mistook Nat's imitation of anger for the real thing.

"And you!" Nat pointed at the boy. "You come here right now!"

Tim came reluctantly, his uncertainty growing by leaps and bounds. Jake's laughter tapered off.

As Tim drew near, Nat kept her back to Jake and gave the boy a wide grin. "Help me catch him."

His face awash with relief, Tim grinned back and nonchalantly edged his way toward his uncle. Once the boy had clasped Jake's hand, Nat sprang, too. Amidst a great deal of shouting and threatening and pleading for mercy, she and Tim pushed, pulled, and shoved him toward the lawn sprinkler.

Well aware Jake could effortlessly break free of them

at any time, that he was just playing along with them, Nat strengthened her determination to have revenge.

Forcing him into the spray, though, was like trying to topple a solid fortress with her bare hands. She and Tim got him within a foot of the spray and could get him no farther. Changing her strategy, she gave up, saying to Tim, "Actually, it feels kind of good."

She jumped into the stream of shooting water and dared Tim to follow. He was only too eager. They danced and laughed and insisted the water wasn't the least cold, but Jake was no fool—he wasn't falling for their little trickery, at least not fully clothed.

Nat abandoned that plan and, careful to calculate her fall, slumped to the ground. She held her head between her hands, doing her best to look suddenly stricken by whatever calamity might strike a person foolish enough to get overheated, then stand beneath a stream of cold water.

Tim was beside her in an instant, his young voice full of concern. "Natalie! Are you sick? What's wrong?"

Careful not to lift her gaze from the ground, she said brokenly, "I don't know. I just feel kind of... lightheaded all at once. I'll be all right in a minute."

"Come off it, Nat," Jake jeered. "That isn't going to work. Get off the ground before you drown."

Paying him no heed, she said in a weakening voice, "Is it getting dark, Tim? Oh dear...I think...I'm going to...fai-n-n...."

Tim gave her a shake, then screeched, "Uncle Jake, she isn't teasing. She really did faint!"

Far less sure of himself, Jake nonetheless muttered dark threats under his breath as he stepped into the circle of falling water to kneel at her side. It was an ir-rational panic that gripped him. He knew it even as he formed his blustery words.

"For your sake, Nat Franklin, you'd better have fainted. Because if this is just a stunt, so help me, I'll..."

Her soft moan increased the pressure building in-side him—if she'd really fainted... His heart beating in a sudden frantic race, he scooped her off the wet grass. She lay limply in his arms and moaned again when he eased her to a dry stretch of ground.

"Should I have Grandma call a doctor?"

Tim's voice sliced through the numbness that fet-tered his ability to act. "Wait a second, Tim, till I take her pulse."

Jake captured her slim wrist and pressed it with his fingertips—her pulse was racing to beat the band. Growing skeptical once again, he watched her eyes flutter open, heard her teasing "Gotcha, didn't I?" and wanted more than anything to shake the breath out of her.

Tim, on the other hand, clapped his hands and chortled. "She did, Uncle Jake! She got you!"

"Natalie Franklin, I ought to spank you!" Jake growled. He dropped her wrist, jumped to his feet, and glowered down at her.

Nat, looking a little bit hurt, stood up and accused him. "You're a sore loser, Jake. I never would have sus-pected it of you."

"That wasn't funny—it was in poor taste. You scared me!"

They were suddenly glaring at one another, Jake genuinely shaken, if not furious, and Nat bewildered.

Only Tim seemed to be deriving any pleasure from the moment. Unaware of the sudden tension in the air, he'd hopped back into the wet spray and was howling out a rowdy song. And even his fun was short-lived, for Hannah poked her head out the door and called him to come in and do his homework.

"Aw, Grandma, tomorrow's Sunday. I don't have to do my homework tonight."

"Yes, you do, young man, and get out of that water before you make yourself sick!" Hannah's eyes flicked over Natalie and Jake. She shook her head. "I'd think grown folks would have better sense."

Tim hastened to obey his grandmother, and Jake, too, turned and strode off without a backward glance. Feeling small and forlorn, a little bit hurt, and very homely in her dripping-wet clothes, Nat slipped into her sandals, walked over the first hill, and confident she was out of view of the house sat down to wring the water out of her hair and dress.

She picked up a stone and tossed it toward the dirt track the farm hands followed to the field. Uncertain that what she felt for Jake was love, she was still starkly aware of her vulnerability. At times she was so in tune with him. They laughed and were carefree, her soul soaring on weightless wings. And tonight, when he'd been hurt by Harold's words, she'd wanted to fight for him, she'd been so incensed.

She needed a clearer vision of where Jake entered in. He treated her with the affection of an older brother, and if she persisted in letting her imagination roam over a dream future, she was going to end up brokenhearted. It was that simple. She hadn't come here to fall in love, she'd come to write a book. She sat a while longer, her thoughts turning to communion with God. *Help me, Lord, to keep my priorities straight,* she ended her prayer. Before she could become any colder, she got to her feet and strolled back to the house.

Chapter Five

The golden glow of Sunday wrapped the Brandon household in tentative peace. Natalie came to the breakfast table dressed in an apricot gauze-cloth dress, smocked and snugly fitted at the bodice then falling to her knees in loose folds. She was thin enough to wear it well and was aware of Jake's quick glance of male interest. *That's all it is,* she warned a stirring heart.

She might have paid him the same compliment, for he was a fine figure in his dress clothes, even without his suit jacket. His complexion made a dark contrast to his white shirt. His hair was still damp from the shower, and he smelled of soap and a tangy after-shave.

As they all gathered for Hannah's bountiful breakfast, his smile could not have been more beguiling. "Let's see," he mused, "this is Sunday. I guess we both seat ourselves, eh?"

She had to curb her smile at the reminder of yesterday's banter. If she was to gird herself against his charm, she had to stop melting like butter at every look, every smile, every word.

Despite the presence of both brothers, the meal was

pleasant. Harold aimed no barbed remarks at Jake, and he didn't harp on Timothy's table manners. Marianne was looking forward to hearing a guest minister that morning, and even Hannah seemed in an agreeable mood, inquiring without complaining about the wet shirt she'd found tossed over a chair in the living room the evening before.

Jake confessed ownership. Then Timothy related Natalie's trick to lure Jake into the path of the lawn sprinkler. He drew a good laugh over Jake's getting doused. Apparently Jake had gotten over his annoyance of the night before, for he chuckled right along with the rest of them and admitted Nat was one up on him.

He did not seem to hold it against her, though, for before the meal ended, he asked, "Are you coming to church with us this morning, Nat, or are you still trying on hats?"

His eyes twinkled with private laughter, for a week earlier he had accused her of trying out the area churches like a woman shopping for a new hat.

Nat struck a demure pose, folding her hands in her lap and lifting her chin. "There's one little pillbox on the edge of town I haven't tried yet. And if I'm going to make it on time, I'd better hurry." She scooted back her chair. "Don't plan on me for lunch, Hannah. I plan to get a sandwich in town, then change clothes and go roaming."

"Roaming where?" Tim piped up, face alive with interest.

Nat placed her folded napkin on the table and remained vague. "I don't know for sure, Tim. Everyone has been praising the beauty of the Shawnee National

Forest. Maybe I'll drive down that way to do my hiking."

"Oh boy! That sounds like fun. Can I go, too?" Tim nearly tipped his chair over in his frenzy to be included.

"Timothy, you weren't invited," Hannah jumped in before Harold could reprimand the boy.

To soften Tim's disappointment, Marianne chimed in. "Your father is going to be home for the next week or so, Tim. Maybe the two of you could work in some hiking."

Pleased by Harold's agreement, Nat left the house. She hated to leave Tim out, but with so much on her mind, she needed to be alone for a time.

She was halfway to the garage when Jake stepped out on the veranda and called after her, "Wait a minute, Natalie. I'll back your car out."

Mildly piqued, Nat waited for his long stride to close the distance between them. "Do you have such a poor opinion of my driving, you don't think I can get the car out of the garage?"

"Tut, tut," he scolded. "I try to be a gentleman, and what do I get? Suspicion cast upon my motives. I'm not doubting your ability—I'm saving you the trouble. Give me your keys."

She deposited the keys in his outstretched hand. "Just as long as you're not doubting me."

She stood to one side, waiting as the automatic garage door yawned open and her blue Pinto backed out onto the drive. Jake climbed out but temporarily blocked her from getting in by standing in the open door.

"You know, I could go with you," he said.

"To church? I think not." She fashioned a quick

excuse. "You don't have your suit jacket, and I don't have time to wait."

"I didn't mean to church. I meant this afternoon. I'm footloose and fancy-free. Where did you say you're doing your hiking?" Though the question was evenly phrased, his eyes were alert.

"Shawnee National Forest. Why?"

With a pained expression, he drawled, "Care to be a little more specific? There's 250,000 acres to that forest, and I don't think you plan to cover it all in one afternoon."

She had not made any specific plans, wanted merely to have an afternoon alone. Yet as he stood before her, boyishly entreating, she found it difficult to turn down his company.

"You needn't worry, Jake," she said finally. "I'm not going to drag you along and make you climb all the hills and exclaim over the scenery. I know it's old hat to you, but it's new and exciting to me."

When his gaze met with hers, she saw a fresh frankness in the blue of his eyes. "In other words, you aren't in the mood for any company."

She flushed and caught her lip between straight white teeth. "I don't mean to be ungracious, Jake, but—"

"You could never be that," he interrupted and grinned when her blush deepened.

"It's just that I'm having a little trouble with my book...."

"The history book?"

"No, my saga—the book I work on in my spare time. Anyway, I've come to an impasse, and I thought if I—"

"How true to life! We all encounter an impasse at

some time or other," he interrupted again.

Her posture erect, she motioned him out of her way and slid beneath the wheel of the blue Pinto. "As I was saying, I'm having a little trouble with the plot of my story. And I thought if I could spend the afternoon alone, walking it out, so to speak, I might come up with a solution."

"I've heard, in such cases, if you focus in on something seemingly minor and build on it, you can find a way out. But then, fiction, even historical fiction, has never been my forte."

Her mind seized the idea as good advice, for her story at least. It seemed risky for a real-life situation, though. "I'll give it some thought. You could be right."

He leaned in the open window. "Nat? Be careful, will you? I really don't like the idea of your roaming around all by yourself. In this day and age—"

"Come now, Jake, I'm a big girl." She took her turn at interrupting him.

His eyes swept her face, an alarming tenderness flickering in their depths. "I know. That's what worries me. Take one more piece of advice, will you Nat? Choose an area where there are lots of people. Garden of the Gods, for instance. The rock formations are fascinating, and there are plenty of nature trails."

Touched by his concern, she agreed. "Okay, Garden of the Gods it is."

She drove off, her heart throbbing so loudly in her ears, she nearly missed his call after her to be home by dinner or he'd come looking for her.

She stilled the foolish pulsing of blood to her head. The warning was indicative of his brotherly protectiveness. He would have expressed no less concern for his mother or Hannah, so she needn't get all worked up imagining an intimacy not intended.

The Shawnee National Forest was every bit as awe-inspiring as promised. Heavy forest covered hills and valleys. Lakes were plentiful and so were gigantic rock arrangements.

A geological upheaval and the gradual influence of wind and water had sculpted the rocks into a recreational attraction now known as Garden of the Gods. Flagstone paths wound through the rock formations, giving easy visual access to such landmarks as Anvil Rock, Buzzard Roost, and Camel Rock.

Nat found herself tempted by the more rugged dirt paths which weaved through the hills. But heeding Jake's warnings, she stayed on the flagstone paths and tagged along behind a hearty-looking elderly couple who read so loudly from their guide sheet she seldom needed to glance at her own.

She ambled along, knitting the plot over the trouble spot in her novel, ripping out stitches, then rejoining it more deftly. She also worked on her problem with Jake. Even without Hannah's advice, she'd known Jake was not interested in her in that special way that lifted a man-woman relationship beyond physical attraction, that fused a couple together heart, body and soul.

In her weeks at the Brandon house, precious little had been said about Jake's wife, Gina. But Jan, Harold's wife, was mentioned with warmth and frequency. This contrast led Nat to wonder if Jake's marriage had not been such a success. Yet it seemed Jake still grieved over Gina's death. Nat was left fluctuating between thinking Jake would never remarry because he had lost faith in the institution and believing he would not remarry because he could never love another woman as much as he'd loved Gina.

This much she knew of Gina—she'd been a stunning beauty with a successful modeling career. During the years of the marriage New York had been home base, with Jake frequently flying off on foreign news assignments. The fatal accident had occurred after a visit to Sutton Valley Estate. A lucrative modeling assignment had come up unexpectedly, and in Gina's haste to return home, she'd chartered a small private plane to Chicago where she could connect with a flight to New York.

At Gina's invitation, Jan had gone along, planning to get in some shopping in New York. Tragically the plane had run into a sudden thunderstorm over central Illinois and crashed. The pilot and both passengers had been killed on impact.

Tim lost a mother, Hannah a daughter, Marianne two daughters-in-law. And Harold and Jake both lost their wives. Nat could not help wondering if the reason for Harold's coldness toward his brother lay somewhere therein. Though the sun was hot on her bare arms, the thought made Nat shiver. Did Harold blame Jake for his wife's death?

Realizing she was no longer thinking about her book at all but delving into others' problems, she gave herself a mental shake. It was late afternoon and she should start back. But first she planned on feeding a pay phone a handful of coins and enjoying a lengthy visit with her mother and whoever else happened to be around.

The peaceful beauty of the Garden of the Gods plus her mother's welcome voice left Natalie so tranquil she dawdled on her way home and nearly missed dinner.

If Jake had begun to worry, he hid it well, giving her little more than a cursory, "How was your afternoon?" Then he announced to the family that he'd be leaving right after dinner to follow a lead on a story he'd been writing.

"Will you be gone long, Jake?" Marianne's concerned glance traveled from Jake to her elder son, then back to Jake again.

"I don't know, Mother. A week perhaps. It's hard to say."

Timothy was subdued; Hannah glowered like a poison toad. Nat studied the circle of faces, wondering if more than a story lead was spiriting Jake away. Had he and Harold tangled again?

Anxious to hold fast to the serenity of the day and hoping to avoid a quarrel, Nat manipulated the conversation, sharing her day at the Garden of the Gods as she helped Hannah clear the dishes away.

Yet once in the kitchen and alone with Hannah she was overcome by curiosity. Submerging her hands in hot sudsy water, she asked the grim-lipped housekeeper, "What's wrong with Harold?"

Not the least fooled by her roundabout approach, Hannah grunted irritably. "He's got a jealous spirit. Mark my word, there's nothing so ugly as a jealous spirit."

Unless it was a cross one. Nat stole a swift sideglance at Hannah's stern mouth and wondered if she dared delve any deeper.

"Did he and Jake quarrel?"

"Can't hardly call it a quarrel when Harold does all the yapping and Jake just stands there and takes it."

"Perhaps Jake understands a harsh answer will only make matters worse."

Hannah gave a haughty sniff as she elbowed her way up to the sink and took over the washing. "Don't misunderstand, I'm a churchgoing woman. But sometimes turning the other cheek seems purely addle-headed. Today, for instance. Harold closed himself into the library to work on a speech. Tim found his Uncle Jake, and the two of them went fishing. When they got back, Harold railed at Jake it might be nice if he could get a chance at his son, seeing how he'd been away so much lately.

"All Jake said was, 'Sorry, Harold. Tim didn't mention the two of you had plans.' Now I ask you, can you beat that, Natalie? I'd have torn Harold up like a paper sack, if it'd been me."

And that she would, Nat thought, hard-pressed not to sympathize with her sentiments. Yet Hannah's attitude saddened her, too. The faithful in Christ needed to uphold, not undermine, His teachings.

Jake seemed to maintain a remarkable calm in the face of his brother's unjust comments. That gave Nat the courage to say to Hannah, "You know, I admire Jake for his patience with Harold. Think how upset Marianne would be if Jake came back with a smart answer every time Harold got unpleasant. There would never be any peace around here."

Hannah's eyes, though narrowed, were all-seeing. She snorted. "You'd admire Jake for having sense enough to come in out of the rain. And next time you've got a sermonette, just come right out and tell old Hannah you think she could take a lesson from Jake."

"Not from Jake," Nat said softly, "from Scripture."

For a moment, she thought she'd gone too far. Hannah turned on her, eyes blazing. But before a single word of wrath could spill out, Nat caught her hand and squeezed it. "Just food for thought, Hannah. Be a dear now, and don't scold me for saying what I believe."

Hannah turned sharply away but not before Nat saw the quick glisten of tears in her pale eyes. She jutted out a trembly chin and offered her highest words of praise. "Sometimes you remind me of my Jan. She was never afraid to knock me down a peg if she thought it needed doing. Maybe the Lord sent you along to remind me life's not all bitter."

Feeling tears sting her own eyes, Nat gave Hannah a hug. The old woman accepted it awkwardly, then shook herself free. "But don't be getting sure of yourself now, Missy. I still say if you had the sense God gave a goose, you'd hightail it on home. Each day you stay the hurt'll get worse. He thought my Jan was a sweet girl, but that was as far as it went. Watching the two of you is like seeing history repeat itself."

She brushed a sleeve across her eyes, then finished her warning. "If Harold comes to you on bended knee, take my advice—don't walk, run to the nearest exit! That's how it happened with Jan. She saw she could never have Jake, and with Harold wearing her resistance down, she finally settled for him. Not that Harold didn't love her. He did. And he was good to her, too. Maybe Jan even came to love him a little in return. But there was no happy-ever-after ending. And there won't be for you either, if you keep looking starry-eyed at Jake."

Nat's temptation to deny she felt anything for Jake felt cheap. Instead, she kissed Hannah's leathery cheek and whispered, "Thanks for caring. I'll remember the warning."

"Yeah, well, while you're remembering, take yourself on out of my kitchen and let me get on with my work."

Nat sidled out of the kitchen, on through the house, and out the front door into the twilight. It was humiliating to realize her irrepressible love for Jake was so evident. Hannah had known all along. Even as Nat denied it to herself, Hannah had known! If Jake knew, it could be playing a part in his decision to leave for a while. Maybe Hannah was right. Maybe she should leave.

But she'd come here with a job to do. It would be unfair to Marianne, unfair to herself, too, to leave without completing it. And with Jake gone, everything might fall into its proper perspective. Maybe it was just infatuation.

She stood with her back to a veranda pillar watching twilight yield to darkness. As the curtains closed on the day she waited for the first stars to appear in the sky and asked the Lord to give direction to her life.

She heard the door swing open behind her and she turned to see Jake, suitcase in hand, silhouetted in the warm glow of light from the hallway. Then the door closed, and she thought with relief how much easier it was to face him in darkness. She was wearied by the events of the day, her dress was crumpled, and her feet were tired inside her dusty canvas shoes.

Pausing beside Nat at the top of the step, Jake set his suitcase down and reached into his pocket. He pressed a butterscotch into her hand, then unwrapped one for himself.

Enough light remained for her to see him roll the empty wrapper between his hands. The gesture had grown familiar and somehow very dear. She smiled at the taste for butterscotch she'd acquired in the past weeks.

"I thought you'd gone," she said around her piece of candy.

"I would have, but first Tim detained me, then Mother."

And now me, she thought. She picked up his suitcase. "Shall I hail you a taxi?"

He chuckled, his hand temporarily covering hers as he reclaimed the suitcase. "No, but you can walk me to my car."

"As late as it is, you'd do as well to wait until morning." She descended the stairs beside him, her heart stirred by the simple pleasure of walking with him.

"You're probably right, but once I get the urge to go, there's no holding me back."

She read into that a deeper meaning, a gentle warning that her love could not bind him. Cooler, more businesslike, she asked, "And where are you off to this time?"

"Back to have another try at Rhaol-Tech. The president of the company stepped down unexpectedly. We're thinking the incoming fellow might be more open to an interview."

"That's the industrial fumes thing, isn't it? Where the employees keep getting sick?"

He touched the end of her nose as she'd seen him do to Timothy a hundred times and chuckled. "Good memory there, Nat. Too bad you're so tied up here. You could come along for the ride."

She didn't believe him for a second and was hurt. "Thanks, but no thanks. And if I were you, I'd try not to breathe while I was there."

"Breathe or don't breathe, a losing proposition any way you look at it. I'll try to make it a brief interview."

"Do that." Aware she'd spoken more curtly than she'd intended, she felt herself the object of a rather sharp look as they approached the garage.

He tilted his head to one side. "Are you miffed about something?"

"No. Should I be?"

He did not reply, rather swung the walk-in garage door open and hit the light switch and the electric overhead door opener simultaneously.

"So how was the pillbox on the edge of town? You never did say."

"Warm and friendly. And the sermon was in basic English—my brothers' terminology for easily understood."

"And the subject matter?" he asked as he stepped to the rear of the car and opened the trunk.

"Brotherly love." She looked right at him as she said it.

Though he was not by nature indecisive, she saw him hesitate. Would he let the moment pass or would he seize the opportunity to make her understand how it was between him and Harold?

It seemed he would do neither. Rather, after stowing his suitcase in the trunk, he stood, hands on hips, staring at it. Suddenly he turned, and his voice was faintly accusing. "You and Hannah must have had quite a talk out there in the kitchen."

"It was you who challenged me to make a friend of her."

His mouth softened. "In her own gruff way, she likes you, you know."

83

"Yes, I know. She told me tonight I sometimes remind her of her daughter."

Again, surprise broke through his cautious expression. "You *did* have quite a talk. So what questions has she planted in that busy mind of yours?"

"You won't bark at me if I ask?"

His eyes seemed a midnight blue as they roamed her features in the poorly lit garage. He reached out a hand to run a thumb along the smooth texture of her cheek.

"Have I ever?" he asked. And he pulled her near, bringing her head to rest upon his shoulder.

Mesmerized by the beat of his heart, she lifted her face, then brought a hand up to brush a wayward curl off his forehead without stopping to think. "Jake, why does Harold take verbal digs at you all the time?"

It wasn't the question he'd expected. She could see that in the shifting pattern of his face. He forced her face against his chest again and resettled his chin into the nest of her hair.

"Ask me something easy, Nat. Like why Harold doesn't want you to write the Sutton history. Or why Mother locks the staircase to the tower room."

Those questions had occurred to her, too, though she'd never been bold enough to ask them. Right now, they were secondary. She wanted to know why Jake was so reluctant to speak of Harold's shabby treatment.

"Does it have something to do with his wife's death, Jake?" she whispered, as if doing so would somehow make the question less offensive.

His fingers tunneled through her hair and caused a whole riot of new emotions within her. "I don't know," he murmured. "Maybe. Yes."

He fell silent. Fearing he would say no more, bring her no closer to understanding, she implored, "Tell me, Jake. Won't you please? I don't want to dislike him, but I do. If I could understand what makes him behave the way he does, then I could pray for him with a more sincere heart."

"Don't be too hard on him, Nat." His breath stirred her hair. "I never was content to let him get the lion's share of attention. There was always a lot of competition between us. Even though he was ahead of me in school, whatever he excelled in, I had to equal or surpass. I'm not proud of it, but it's the truth.

"Mother did give me the right name, after all. I've been the biblical Jacob struggling with his brother Esau. Not for the birthright—I've never wanted the farm. But I did take his girlfriend. He brought her home to meet Mother, and I married her."

Stunned in spite of herself—it seemed so unlike the Jake she knew and adored—she stepped back from him. A chill sliced through her and she chafed her arms. "Gina?"

"Gina."

"Jake, that was low."

"What? You've never heard 'All's fair in love and war'?"

It was as if she'd been wrong, as if she neither knew nor understood the true Jake Brandon at all.

Covering the crack in her composure with the grace of honesty, she backed toward the door. "Yes, I've heard it said. But I can't say I've ever believed it."

Her eyes held his for only a moment before she slipped back out into the comforting darkness of the night.

Despite her wrinkled dress and tousled hair, there was a quiet dignity about her, Jake thought as he watched her go, resisting the urge to remind her he'd already said he wasn't proud of the way he'd behaved. He'd been self-centered and headstrong, a token Christian more interested in taking his place on the Friday night church bowling team than in the Sunday morning worship.

He hadn't intended to tell her things he'd told no other living soul. When she'd come to him with questions in her green eyes, he'd foolishly assumed she'd ask him for the truth about old Jacob Sutton's reputation, the slavery thing. Ever since she'd come, he'd been waiting, anticipating, wondering when she would realize old Jacob wasn't all he was cracked up to be.

But then, who is? he thought. He slammed down the trunk lid. He was accustomed to living with the things he'd done to Harold as a young and ambitious and terribly self-centered man. But the shock of it reflected by her fresh innocence brought the disgust flowing over him in waves.

But Christ's blood covered those sins he'd confessed the day he finally realized he was married to a woman as shallow and self-centered as he was. He'd poured out all his unhappiness in prayer and humbly committed himself to the Christian walk. From that day on, he'd accepted Gina as she was. They were indeed in it together, for better or worse.

When he'd come home from a special assignment in El Salvador to learn she was pregnant, he'd been overjoyed. Maybe a child couldn't save a marriage, but perhaps a child linked with his rediscovered faith could.

Or so he'd hoped. Gina was peevish about it. A baby wasn't in her plans. But he humored her along, got her to go home with him to tell his mother the good news. For one week their marriage had seemed good.

Then the phone call came: a "once in a lifetime" modeling opportunity. She seized it, fearing her modeling days would soon be over. He hadn't wanted her to go, but finally he agreed she could fly back and he'd join her after he drove the car back.

In some way he could not define, Jan's going along with her had damaged his already scarred relationship with his brother beyond repair. Most of the time, he let whatever Harold had to say flow in one ear and out the other. But Harold's sneering about his not having a child did hurt. Especially when Harold knew how excited he'd been over the baby....

"Jake?"

He jerked his head around to find Natalie back. She paused, hand on the passenger's door, eyes round and anxious, bottom lip caught between her teeth.

"What is it?" he asked over the roof of the car.

"I hope I didn't...that is, I didn't mean to sound so...It wasn't as if they were engaged or anything. They weren't, were they?"

"No."

She smiled at him. He gripped the door handle hard, jerking it open. That smile of hers went through him like a volley of shots. Shaken by his unexpected thoughts of sunshine and violets, spring showers' freshness and rainbows, he slid into the car vowing to sort it all out. He'd been gliding along, enjoying their friendship, never scratching beneath the surface. Maybe it was time he took a closer look.

He heard the passenger door open and turned as she settled onto the seat. She folded her hands in her lap and shot him an apprehensive glance. "I didn't hurt your feelings, did I?"

He looked at her blankly. "What are you doing?"

He sensed rather than saw the rush of color to her cheeks. She murmured casually, "I thought I'd ride to the end of the lane with you, then walk back. You don't mind, do you?"

"Yes, I mind. I stayed around all day just to be sure you got home all right, and now you want to go wandering around in the dark. What's the matter with you, anyway?"

He saw her chew her lip again, knew she was miserable, and couldn't imagine why he'd lashed out at her or why he now wanted to smooth her hair back from her face and kiss that lip she was so bent upon bruising with her teeth.

"I don't know, I just thought the walk would do me good. That sounds silly, doesn't it? I walked all afternoon. I'm tired, too, but I'm not sleepy, if you know what I mean."

He knew what she meant all right, had ached with weariness many a night and never shut an eye. But he also knew if he weakened he'd end up kissing her and not just a light friendly peck on the cheek either. And that would change everything. They'd never be able to go back to the easy, no-demands relationship he'd been enjoying.

He backed out of the garage, then pulled around and stopped in front of the house. "Read a book, Natalie, or watch television or plot out your next chapter. But don't wander around in the dark and don't ask for more than I can give."

This time she asked no questions, just climbed out of the car soundlessly and, with slim shoulders held very straight, walked away without looking back.

Chapter Six

So much for honesty, Nat thought, humiliation holding sway as she blinked back her tears and climbed the stairs to her room. For centuries, women in love had been delaying good-byes, accompanying the men of their dreams to gateposts at the edges of yards, to railway stations, to airports to prolong the moment of parting.

Heart in her hand, she'd asked to go to the end of the lane with him, and he'd turned her down, eager to be off unfettered by any brotherly concern about whether she made it back to the house safely. That in itself hurt enough. But then those blue eyes of his had cut past her flimsy excuse of needing a walk before bed. They'd tunneled beneath her hastily donned mask of mere friendship. They'd seen to the truth in her soul.

Don't ask for more than I can give. He couldn't have made himself any clearer. She snatched up her gown and robe and went to the bathroom for a shower, wishing the cleansing water could wash away the ache and humiliation of rejection.

She reasoned that time would dull the pain, but as

the days passed, the hurt didn't lessen. Instead, she missed Jake with building intensity. Work didn't help. Summer vacation and Timothy's bids for her attention didn't help. Hannah's treating her to Hannah-style tenderness, clucking and fussing because she picked at her food and spent too much time closed up in the tower room, didn't help. Nor did the daily invasion of Harold's loud and energetic campaign staff.

When after a week Jake had neither returned nor bothered to phone, she spent another afternoon in Shawnee National Forest. This time she roamed a rugged dirt path through a secluded stretch of tree-covered hills. It was a childish defiance of Jake. And it was nonsensical in terms of both safety and logic—but he wasn't around to worry or care.

Someone did care, though—Hannah. On Natalie's return at dusk, Hannah bit into her arm with bony fingers and propelled her toward the kitchen sink. "Wash your hands and face, and sit down at the counter while I fix you a bite to eat."

"Don't bother. I'll just bathe and go on to bed," Nat said, too exhausted to care about food.

"Oh no you won't! You wash and sit down. I know you've been wandering off by yourself all day. Good thing the Lord looks after those who are too lame-brained to look after themselves."

With a guilty downsweep of her lashes, Nat did as she was told, but Hannah's tirade went on. "Missing lunch isn't enough. You go and miss supper, too. I don't expect you to care about making extra work for me. But you ought to care about what you're doing to yourself. Have you looked in the mirror lately, Missy?"

With her face hidden in a towel, Nat's "I said you didn't have to fix me anything" came out muffled.

"Well, maybe you haven't noticed, but you're turning into a skeleton. Startin' tomorrow you're going to eat right and get some sunshine. And I don't mean stuffed-up sun in that tower either. It's too blamed hot up there, and you know it. It'll drain the life right out of you."

"But—"

"Now you sit down and eat. Then off to bed with you and no sitting up late reading, either. I've seen the light under your door."

Nat's head was beginning to ache from the attack. "Don't fuss, Hannah," she pleaded.

"Somebody'd better fuss, you with your big eyes spilling all over your face. Marianne thinks you've lost your taste for your job, Timothy thinks you don't love him anymore, and Harold—well, he's too busy campaigning to think. But you aren't fooling me, Missy. I know you're grieving. Didn't I warn you? Didn't I?"

Feeling like a thoroughly chastened child, Nat hung her head and said nothing.

"We both know I did! 'Course it's not the first time my good advice went unheeded. Eat now, you hear? Then go on to bed. There's going to be some changes around here tomorrow. Mark my word!"

Hannah marched off toward the door. Swallowing the lump in her throat, Natalie called her name. She turned back, and Nat swallowed again, wanting to thank her, to tell her she had heard every word and deserved it, too. But she knew if she tried, the tears would spill. Hannah continued to wait, kindness and anxiety under her habitual impatience.

"You don't suppose you could find me one of your butterscotch cookies, do you?"

Hannah's face softened. "Dear Lord, what am I

going to do with you, child?"

"Is he coming back, Hannah?"

"Of course he is. He always does."

Nat blinked hard on her tears. "I thought maybe I'd made it uncomfortable for him. If I'm keeping him away, then I'll leave. This is his home, not mine."

"Don't be silly. He's just got tied up with his work that's all. It's not unusual for him to be gone for a month or two. And about those cookies—I'll bake some tomorrow. You eat your fill. Then we'll freeze the rest for when he comes home."

Nat gave her a watery smile. "Thanks, Hannah."

"Nothing to thank me for. Cooking's my job," Hannah said with a sniff, as if she did not know it was her staunch support for which Natalie was grateful.

Nat watched her go, wondering how she could have ever felt anything but fondness for Hannah and her mixed-up mixture of love and frustration, gruffness and kindness.

She ate her dinner slowly, knowing Hannah was right. So Jake would never be anything more than a friend. He made a good friend, a friend to be treasured. And his family was a confusing bunch, but a caring bunch, too, and she was richer for the experience. Her research was nearing completion.

She'd longed for a way to show Harold he was missing a lot by not getting to know his brother. He'd probably laugh, a bitter, jealous laugh. Jake was a man worth knowing.

Later, in the moonglow through the curtains at her bedroom window, Natalie emptied her heart to God. It was He who'd designed the attraction between man and woman. Who better to understand the overwhelming emotions sweeping her into such despair?

But He was also a healer, and it was for emotional healing she prayed. Her prayers were also for Jake, for the members of his family, for Hannah. She wanted so much to see Hannah become a happier person, unafraid to trust in love.

She slept a deep, restful sleep and awakened at dawn, pleasantly enveloped in a dream of Jake. Choosing to be thankful rather than regretful, she lay very still until the realness of it faded. Then she rose to start afresh.

As she went through the day, she realized quite a lot had been slipping by her during the week. To keep clear of Harold's campaigning staff, Marianne had taken an interest in Hannah's garden. Watching their working figures, Nat formed a smile. They looked so companionable.

Tim, on the other hand, was bored. Nat watched him out in the yard all alone, tossing a ball up and catching it. She looked at her desk and hesitated, thinking of her plans to start on the rough draft of the history. But her softness for the child won out, and she took an hour off and walked down to the deer park with him. It was a walk she and Jake had often taken but always at dusk when the deer were grazing.

On the way back Tim chatted incessantly about his hike with his father last Saturday. Chagrined, Nat realized she hadn't even missed him.

But the biggest surprise came midafternoon when Hannah called her down from the tower for lemonade and cookies, butterscotch cookies! Harold joined them in the kitchen and with him a lovely young woman he introduced as Rose Mulvanich, a volunteer campaigner.

They visited long enough for Nat to gather pretty

Rose might be campaigning for something personal as well as for a senator. After they'd gone, Nat winked at Hannah and whispered, "Does love bloom in little Rose's eyes?"

Hannah turned a morose face on her and muttered, "Lord preserve us. What next?"

But as the days passed, Nat found Rose was a lovely young woman and honest, too. She made no attempt to bribe Timothy. Nor did she deny it when Hannah accused her pointblank of husband hunting. If Nat hadn't come to love Hannah so much, she might have been tempted to strangle her for being so rude.

The early history of old Jacob Sutton was coming along well, and the rough draft shaped up. Nat had uncovered a puzzle, though, something to do with Jacob's only daughter, and another week passed as she sought in vain to solve it. It began to look as if she'd have to make a trip to town for a look at the files in the county courthouse. She wanted to find out what had become of Oreana Sutton, Jacob's only daughter.

Yet when Nat mentioned it to Marianne, Marianne appeared startled, then vague. "It's such a minor point, Natalie. Why don't you just forget it?"

But Natalie could not. Oreana, "Annie" as she was known to her family, was the youngest child and the only daughter of the Suttons. She had kept a diary and though it was done in the hit-and-miss fashion common to children, it provided valuable insight into the home life of the first generation of Suttons to grow up in the valley.

At age eight, Annie had written in wobbly letters of the house "bumpin and creakin in the night." Having spent some late-night hours in the tower, Nat had smiled in sympathy over that entry, for the house did have its peculiar noises. Further, the little girl had written of her father's soothing her fears, even going out to the well to bring her a cup of cold water. The next day she'd noted her father had rebuked her older brothers for tormenting her with tales of ghosts and goblins.

It was such a tender picture of Jacob Sutton. It seemed to Nat he'd been bigger in the eyes of his daughter than he was in the respectful eyes of his neighbors and business peers. Perhaps it was fanciful of her to endow old Jacob with some of the same fine qualities she admired in Jake. And yet, why not? After all these years, Jacob's personality was almost purely a matter of speculation, and Marianne wanted a personal, living account.

Marianne liked the passages she'd shared with her thus far, all dealing with Jacob as a young man. Something nagged at Natalie, though, a memory of Jake's discomfort with bearing the name of old Jacob Sutton.

She continued to wrestle with that problem throughout June, the month of gentle morning showers, sunny afternoons carrying the scent of fresh-mown grass and sweet corn tassels, and hopefully Jake's homecoming.

Climbing the stairs to the darkened tower room for an extra hour or two of research had become a habit. She wondered if searching the same old papers over for a line on Annie Sutton wasn't a futile waste of time. Yet she continued, for it seemed less foolish than retiring early to drive off fantasies of Jake.

The tower was cool and quiet at night, except for the yawning and creaking of old wood and the whisper of a light breeze at the windows.

Annie's diary ended abruptly after her sixteenth birthday. Even her death notice a few years later denied her a personal identity, referring to her as the only daughter of the county's most successful pioneer, Jacob Sutton. Her husband was mentioned, too, his prominence in Illinois agriculture liberally praised.

But there was no mention of the fact that Annie's land had enabled him to make his achievements. Natalie vented her irritation by closing the last of the scrapbooks less than gently. Dust tickled her nose and she covered a sneeze. It was unfair. Annie had been so overshadowed by her father and her husband she ceased to be Annie.

Natalie leaned back in her chair and rubbed her eyes. A good night's sleep would bathe away the gritty feeling. Her shoulders ached from long hours of poring over research material. But it was discouragement that really weighed her down.

At the sound of brisk footsteps ascending the stairs, she turned, wondering who was still up at this late hour. Timothy wasn't allowed in the tower, and rarely did anyone else bother her here.

The strange stir of hope in her heart intensified to a joyous leap as Jake's tall, broad-shouldered form filled the doorway. The blue of his shirt seemed to catch and intensify the blue of his eyes as he asked, with a dimpled grin, "Aren't you going to welcome me home?"

A ghost of a smile slipped past her guarded reserve. "Welcome home, Jake."

Fishing a handful of candy wrappers out of the pocket of his navy dress slacks, he came toward her. "So did you miss me?"

Still seated behind the table, she let her gaze climb his muscled body to rest on the craggy contours of his face. The warm glow of his eyes, the tumble of curls, his special way of smiling—she'd missed everything about him! But it was not fair of him to ask, not after his unmistakable warning not to ask for more than friendship.

Her happiness mixed with the pain of hopeless loving, she kept her reply as light as her smile. "I guess we all did. Even Hannah, though she'll no doubt deny it."

Was her answer a disappointment? Or was he frowning over his empty pocket? Depositing the pile of wrappers on her makeshift desk—within a foot of the wastepaper basket—he complained, "Fresh out."

"Hannah's baked cookies. They're in the freezer."

"Hannah's a good one. Shall we go help ourselves?"

"Better wait until they're offered," Nat warned, not wanting to deprive Hannah of that pleasure.

"Then let's go down and drop a hint or two."

"I imagine she's gone to bed."

"And everyone else as well. The house was dark when I came up the lane. With the exception of the tower. Were you waiting up for me, or just burning the midnight oil?" Fine crinkle lines fanned out from his eyes.

"Don't flatter yourself. What point would there have been in waiting, anyway? You didn't tell anyone you were on your way home."

At the note of censure in her voice, he tugged at a loose strand of her hair and chuckled. "Are you scolding me, Nat Franklin?"

"No. Though it wouldn't have hurt you to let your mother know you were still alive and well. She's been concerned. Don't you ever write or call when you're gone?"

"I guess I got out of the habit. In the past, I've often

felt she was better off not knowing much about my assignments."

He rested one lean hip on a corner of the table as he abruptly changed the subject. "Anything interesting going on while I was gone?"

She tried to suppress the pleasure of his nearness so she could remember the high points of the past few weeks. "Not much, really. Timothy's bored with summer vacation already. Your mother has taken a sudden interest in gardening, probably due to Harold's turning the library into a campaign headquarters. Oh, and I think Harold has a sweetheart."

"Rose Mulvanich?"

"How'd you know?"

"Rose is a piece of his past. How's Mother taking all the coming and going?"

"It drove her a little crazy at first, but when she realized he was doing it to be nearer to Timothy, she seemed to approve."

"That's a surprise, Harold considering Timothy for a change."

"Maybe you don't know him as well as you think you do, Jake," she suggested gently.

"That could be true. But I've learned the best way for me to get along with Harold is to stay out of his life."

"Have you ever thought, Jake, that you might bring the past into the open with Harold, let him know you regret the division between you? Who knows? It might go a long way toward healing broken ties."

She caught her breath, half expecting him to flare up and order her to mind her own business. But he didn't. Rather, he left his perch, came up from behind,

100

and leaned down to ask, "Why is it you take every-one's troubles to heart, Nat?"

His breath touched her ear, his sandy cheek brushed her smooth one, and her heart went curving, twisting, twirling. Not trusting herself to answer, she straightened her spine, pushed her chair back, and went to the nearest window to peer out at the black velvet night.

"Life's hard, isn't it?" he said, his voice filling the emptiness of the room with heartfelt discouragement.

She felt humbled, unworthy of answering, for to this point in her life, the hours that had made up her days had never seemed hard. Even knowing how hard her mother had worked for their home, she'd never felt needy or deprived. Perhaps it was the closeness of the family, the love that had sheltered her. Love was free and plentiful as the air she breathed—until now, when she found herself loving a man who'd never love her back.

"I don't know, Jake," she said finally. "Is it?"

He fed the silence for so long she began to think he'd gone, but she lacked the courage to turn and see. There was nothing to see out the window, nothing in the glass but the shadow of her reflection. And then he was just behind her, close enough to touch but not touching.

"I'm afraid I've hurt you," he said softly, his words ragged.

She started to deny it, then changed her mind. "It doesn't matter, Jake."

"But it does. Believe me, I did it unthinkingly. I seem to have a knack for hurting or disappointing those closest to me—Harold, Gina, even Mother. And now you."

"Any hurt I feel I brought on myself," she said, being as honest as she knew how.

"You know, Nat, if you didn't care so much, if you didn't take on others' burdens, if you just looked after yourself, you could go a lifetime and never get hurt."

"Yes, but what a lonely life."

"I don't know, Nat. With Harold and me...and my life with Gina...my career as a newsman, too...it hurt so much to care, and it didn't seem to change anything. So I learned to turn down the volume, to let the world float by and look on from somewhere in the wings. And you know, Nat, it's absolutely painless."

He was so wrong it scared her. Did he actually think pain never showed in his eyes? She'd *seen* it there, felt it's force. Yet it would do no good to tell him he was wrong. He really thought the power to love was gone from him.

She turned with sudden decision. "A coma is painless, too, Jake. And death. But we don't embrace them, do we? No, we embrace life. And nothing in life is any sweeter than love. I'm not ashamed of loving you. Nor do I regret it, even though you won't ever love me back. You needn't feel bad or apologize for not feeling the same. Or worry that you've hurt me. At least I know I'm still alive. What about you Jake? Are *you* still alive?"

His eyes grew stormy, and his tone mingled regret and reproach. "I was afraid you wouldn't understand. Perhaps I shouldn't have come home. I almost didn't, but I wanted a chance to explain. If it's a hardship on you, I'll leave again."

Before the stiff offer was out, she was shaking her head. "No, if anyone leaves, it will be me. This is your home, not mine. And though your mother wants the work done here, it doesn't have to be. I've done most of the research. I have my notes. There's no reason I can't get a room in town and complete the book there."

An uneasy silence grew between them. She could only guess at his thoughts, and it seemed to her from his troubled frown he wasn't pleased with the thought of her leaving. "You needn't try to explain it to your mother. I'll simply let it be known I'd be happier in town."

"And *would* you?"

"If I'm in your way here, then yes, I would."

"Don't put words in my mouth," he snapped. "I didn't say I wanted you gone. In fact, it would be inconvenient for a number of people. Mother depends on you now, to keep her posted on your work."

"Which could be done by phone."

"Hannah enjoys your company. And Timothy, too. We've been good friends, Nat. Can't you stay? Can't we continue to be friends?"

He was so boyishly beseeching, she faltered in her resolve to go. Perhaps she was weak to be willing to accept whatever crumbs he would throw her—friendship, when she wanted much more—but the emotional treadmill she'd been pacing came to an abrupt standstill, and she felt only relief at climbing off.

"All right, Jake. Friends it is. And now, friend to friend, you'll understand if I ask you to run along and let me get back to my work, won't you?"

His sooty lashes descended, and with the laughter

she'd come to expect of him he stilled the vibrations running between them.

"You'd better watch it, Nat. That sounded just like Hannah."

"Did not," she denied.

The soft sound of her laughter rang after him as he descended the stairs. It was good to hear, good to know he'd patched up the breach in their friendship.

And yet, the rush of relief he'd expected didn't come. He still felt the shadow of some nameless dissatisfaction. He tried to dismiss her sweet confession of love as a simple case of infatuation and found to his surprise that he wasn't really sure he wanted to.

He gave a gruff laugh. What an egotist *he'd* turned into, flattered senseless over a green-eyed girl's declaration of love.

Chapter Seven

Friends, Jake had said. An uneasy truce would have been a more accurate definition of their relationship. Natalie lamented that her honesty about her feelings had damaged the spontaneity that had once colored their friendship with such delight.

He was quiet, pensive, not at all like himself. And despite her efforts to remain natural, she could feel the protective shell beginning to form. By unspoken consent, the evening walks, the horseplay, the light banter all halted.

To avoid the strain between them, Nat buried herself in her work, spending long hours on the rough draft of the family history. With July came a heat wave and drought. No longer able to endure the heat of the tower, she moved her office to her bedroom, though sometimes, when the library was empty of Harold and his campaigning, she'd close herself in and enjoy the air conditioning.

Hannah would bring her a tray when she missed a meal or scold her until she came out to eat in the kitchen.

Natalie's search for a clue to what kind of woman

Annie Sutton became was at a standstill. Though the clerk at the county courthouse had been cooperative, as had the people at the local genealogical society, nothing useful had turned up.

Recalling that Annie had mentioned the name of the family doctor after her recovery from scarlet fever, Nat went back through the girl's diary, found the doctor's name again, and ran ads in several genealogical bulletins. A descendant of the good doctor might have some old medical records—hopefully Annie's. If that long shot yielded nothing, she would have to go through the microfilms of old newspapers, searching society columns for a chance glimpse of Annie as a grown woman, the wife of a man prominent in Illinois agriculture.

Despite Marianne's repeated suggestion she not trouble herself over Annie, Nat was too curious about the young woman to leave it alone.

On the positive side, Natalie was encouraged to see a gradual change in the Brandon home. Harold no longer spent mealtimes tossing barbed comments at Jake. Nat didn't know whether to attribute that to Jake, who was showing more interest in Harold's campaign, or to Rose, who usually stayed for dinner. Harold seemed quite fond of Rose and would naturally not want to appear the heel.

Whatever the reason, Natalie was thankful for the change and continued to pray for Jake and Harold. The improvement continued until it grew commonplace for the two brothers to discuss Harold's chances in the upcoming election. They seemed to agree that if he didn't win this time around, he would still have a bright political future. He had youth in his favor, and his name would begin to be linked with his stand on each issue.

Timothy was also benefiting from the more peaceful climate. Often, when he complained of boredom, Jake and Harold joined him in a game or a walk or an impromptu fishing trip.

One evening, when Natalie came out for a breath of fresh air, it was to see Harold, Jake, Rose, and Timothy playing baseball on the grass while Marianne looked on. Marianne patted the chair next to her. "I can't get over the change in them. In a way, it makes me a little edgy. I'm so afraid something will happen to destroy the peace."

"Yes, and that something could be Rose," Hannah muttered, coming out onto the veranda with a tray of cold drinks.

"Rose is a dear," Natalie said in the young woman's defense. But she spoke gently, for she understood it was hard for Hannah to see Rose take her daughter's place as Harold's wife and Timothy's mother.

"Attractive, too. And bright, very bright," Marianne added.

Hannah scowled, her eyes fixed on fair-headed Rose making a mad flight around the bases.

"Ever stop to wonder if it's really Harold she's got her sights set on?" Hannah said in an undertone, and at Marianne's rising eyebrows, she added, "My, but aren't you short of memory!"

Nat was floored, for Hannah's reference was clear. She was about to echo Marianne's, "Don't be silly. Jake isn't the least interested in Rose!" But at that moment, a loud round of laughter drew her attention, and she looked out to see Jake holding Rose just off home plate as Harold ran the ball in from outfield.

"Uncle Jake, that's cheating! Let her go!" Timothy yelled, trying to free his teammate who was only a foot or so from a home run.

Still laughing, Jake hung onto Rose's arm a second longer, and in that second, watching the two of them, Natalie knew a pain so real, so raw, so ravaging, she understood in an instant what had festered in Harold's heart for years. She understood jealousy.

Out on the field, the fleeting moment was past. Jake had released Rose, Timothy was jumping up and down over his teammate's home run, and Harold was congratulating her with a hug. Wearing a grin, Jake turned unexpectedly and caught Natalie's naked stare.

"Natalie!" he said finally, with that constraint she couldn't bear. "I didn't know you'd come out."

I'll just bet you didn't! she wanted to shout. Hannah'd put a glass of lemonade in her hand, and Natalie fought the strong urge to sling it at him, to slam into the house with a resounding bang of the door. Her free hand was clenched into a tight fist, her nails chewing into her palm painfully. The pain felt cleansing compared to the pain within.

She forced her hand open, raked fingers through her loose hair, and observed the polite caution on his features as he approached the steps. "Would you like to play, too, Natalie?" he asked. "Rose and Tim could use another player on their team."

Was he really so obtuse? In jeopardy of spitting out words she'd instantly regret, she shook her head and took a calming sip of her drink.

"No, thanks. I have to get back to work."

But before she could leave, he climbed the veranda steps and called to the ballplayers on the lawn. "Let's take a break. Hannah's made lemonade." With a glass in one hand, he plunked down on the arm of her chair.

Damp curls clinging to a moist forehead, shirt equally dampened by perspiration and molded to the muscled wall of his chest, cheeks ruddy from exertion, he radiated a dangerous male energy. The sight of his brown fingers making prints on the moisture of the glass, the sound of his voice rumbling in her ear, the very scent of him filled her with alarm. She bolted out of her chair so fast it nearly overturned under his weight on the arm.

"Nat!" he called after her, but she kept going. Closing herself into the air-conditioned library, she set the glass of lemonade down, lowered herself into the desk chair, and buried her face in her hands.

She was trembling from the inside out. *Was that how it began with Gina, too?* she wondered. In her mind's eye, she could see it: Harold proudly bringing Gina home to meet his mother. Introducing her to Jake. The innocent lighthearted banter. The fun. Then the mutual attraction, the innocence gone, and poor Harold left wondering what had happened.

Always before, she'd seen everything through Jake's eyes. It hit home now how deeply hurt Harold must have been, especially if he had really loved Gina. Had he gone to the wedding? Of course. Propriety would have demanded it. That must have cut like jagged glass!

She rubbed her thumbs over her eyes. Why was she dragging it all out, examining it, torturing herself? It was in the past and had nothing to do with her. It was one thing to be jealous of a living, breathing beauty like Rose, stupid maybe, but understandable. Being jealous of Jake's dead wife, however, was ridiculous. She positioned unsteady fingers on her typewriter keys, and doggedly retyped a page of rough draft. She was halfway down when the library door opened and Jake stepped in.

Hesitantly, he spoke into the clatter of typewriter keys. "Are you all right, Nat?"

"Of course." Her fingers continued to fly over the keys, her mind never registering the meaning of the words.

When he hesitated again, she paused long enough to say, "I have work to do, that's all."

"You know, Nat, no one expects you to work all the time."

"I just want to be done with it, that's all."

"Why?"

When she didn't answer, he came to stand behind her. She stiffened as his hands rested on her shoulders. A buzzing in her ears rose to a full roar as his thumbs worked at muscles made tight by too many hours over a typewriter. It was bliss and torture at the same time, his hands gently working out the soreness but sparking flames she could not extinguish.

"Quit," she ordered.

"Why?"

"Because I'm trying to work and you aren't helping any."

"Why?"

"Is that all you can say? You sound like a parrot."

"Then answer my question."

Maddened by his reasonable tone, she stilled her fingers on the keys and impatiently tilted her head back until his face hovered over her.

"Which question was that?"

"Why are you in such a big hurry to finish this book

and clear out?" His eyes softened with a compassion that bruised her pride.

"Let's just say I'm homesick. Okay?"

"Is it so hard, Nat?"

"What? The book?" Choosing to misunderstand, she shook her head. "No. It's coming along quite well, actually."

"That isn't what I meant."

"Then be more specific."

"Is *being* here so hard?"

"It's pure pleasure. Can't you tell? Don't I look thrilled with it all?"

His hands tightened on her shoulders, a frown starting to form between his brows. "Don't, Natalie. You don't wear sarcasm well."

The stroke of tenderness in his rebuke hurt more than harshness would have. "Leave me alone, Jake," she said and started typing again.

He circled the desk and stood watching her until she felt compelled to glance up, expecting another question. When he said nothing, just kept watching her with a studied expression, she felt her color rise. Finally she spoke with a mixture of resentment and embarrassment. "Go away. Can't you see I'm busy?"

"I'm sorry. It's just that I was wondering how I could have known you so well a few weeks ago and not know you at all now. I'm sorry that our friendship has changed you."

Her heart throbbed with fresh pain. Nothing about her had changed. But he had changed—he'd become uncomfortable with her. *Which is his problem,* she thought with a surge of resentment.

Pretending to be engrossed with her work, she asked him for the correct spelling of a word. Dutifully, he spelled it, then turned his back on her.

Out of the corner of her eye, she watched him browse through the shelves of books, select one, and stretch out in a chair as if he intended to stay.

She blew out a sigh. "I hate to be rude, but I'm *trying* to work."

He feigned innocent surprise. "Am I bothering you? I'll try to be more quiet."

She gave up trying to get rid of him. True to his word, he was quiet. Over the hum of the air conditioner she heard only the uneven click of her typewriter keys slapping paper.

A long time later he closed his book, returned it to the shelf, and left without speaking a word. Then she missed him.

Weary of typing, she took a pen and scribbled changes in the pages she'd typed. After a bit, she turned off the air conditioner and the lights and wearily took herself off to bed.

The week that followed was fraught with activity and confusion. With county fairs and small town summer festivals getting underway, even mealtimes at the Brandon house had turned into campaign planning sessions. Because Harold wished to be widely represented, supporters would open a party booth at each fair and festival to hand out bumper stickers, buttons, and pamphlets. Harold himself would mingle with the crowds and shake hands.

Timothy was unimpressed with his father as a political figure and spent breakfast, lunch, and dinner trying to coax his grandmother into letting him invite a friend out to the farm for a few days. It became apparent Marianne would have to give in to his pressure if she was ever to know peace again. Natalie took cover under the chatter and confusion and lost herself to her own circling thoughts. Since the evening Jake had joined her in the library, she'd sensed a quiet watchfulness about him. His endearing exuberance had waned until it was all but nonexistent. Even his occasional smiles seemed forced, the dimples she loved hardly showing. *What's troubling him,* she wondered when once or twice she'd felt a searching glance and looked up to find his perplexed blue eyes flickering with self-doubt.

Sometimes she almost dared to hope he was reassessing his feelings for her. But then he'd so pointedly ignore her, fresh pain would whip at her heart, making her reflect on the foolishness of an overactive imagination.

On two more occasions he entered the library in the evening while she was working, once to get a book and quickly depart, the second time to stand reading over her shoulder a moment. Painfully insecure over what his opinion of her talent might be, it was all she could do to keep from throwing her hands over the page and begging him to please, please go away. Instead, she turned in her chair and caught his gaze with an inquiring look. He retreated and did not bother her again.

As the weekend approached, Marianne offered Natalie the opportunity to take a few days off. More than ready for a visit home, Natalie eagerly accepted. She drove home on Saturday, enjoyed her family, and returned late Monday afternoon to find the house deserted. After unpacking, she gave in to the stifling heat and changed into a cool pink seersucker blouse that tied at the shoulders, pink shorts, and sandals before she took her rough draft down to the air-conditioned library.

It quickly became apparent someone had leafed through the manuscript in her absence. Several pages were out of order, and her spelling had been corrected in a couple of places.

Her first thought was Marianne. Yet Marianne had never once mentioned her faulty spelling or marked her manuscript in any way. As she looked over the pages in their new order, there seemed almost a pattern to them, a suggestion that the book might flow better if certain passages were rearranged. It would take another writer to see that. A frown forming, Nat wandered out to the kitchen to fix herself a glass of tea.

She glanced out the kitchen window as she sipped her tea and spied Jake stretched out in the fishnet hammock beneath the shade of a tall, wide-slung oak. No doubt he was the culprit. Her annoyance growing, she stepped out the back door, intent on giving him a lesson in respecting the privacy of others.

However, as she started across the backyard, her steps slowed. How she'd missed him! It struck her like a slow-moving train as she looked at him, sound asleep in the hammock. Shoes carelessly cast off, one toppled on the other. Suit jacket and tie thrown in a heap atop grass struggling to survive in the heat. Black-socked feet crossed at the ankles, shirt open at the neck and untucked from his trousers. Damp curls clinging to a beaded brow. A smile stole to her lips.

Her mission completely forgotten, she plucked a tall-stemmed fluffy dandelion and crept up on soundless feet to touch it to the end of his nose. His mustache twisted. She tickled him again. Both nose and mustache twitched and a soft snore pursed out his lips. Holding back laughter, she ran the dandelion down a cheek rough with five o'clock shadow, and his hand came up in a shooing motion, swatting the gray fluff and scattering the seed on the airless afternoon. She giggled and his eyes jerked open. First irritation at being awakened, then welcome shone in their blue depths.

"So you made it back. Hot day for such a long drive, isn't it?" He swung his legs over to the side of the hammock, rubbed his hands over his eyes, and stretched.

Natalie tossed down the dandelion stem. "Where is everyone?"

"Fair time, remember? Harold rode in a parade yesterday, then bullied us all into going back to shake hands and smile today. My smile got a little ragged, so I came home."

He eyed her iced tea thirstily. She took one more swallow and gave it to him. "How'd the parade go? Did Timothy get to ride in the convertible with him?"

"Oh, yes. You should have been there. He was a celebrity for three and a half blocks. Then he saw them tossing out candy from the float just ahead of them. The next time the car stopped, he bailed out and scrambled around with the rest of the kids, stuffing his pockets full. Harold was furious and didn't dare show it."

As their laughter ran together, he motioned for her to sit down beside him. But hammocks weren't made for sitting at a safe distance—she slid right down next to him.

Seeming untroubled by her closeness, he drained the glass of tea. Without looking directly at her, he asked, "How was your time off?"

"Fun. Mom got the whole family together for a picnic after church yesterday. We went swimming, and we all got sunburned, except for the kids. They were already brown as little beavers."

She was rambling and knew it. But her heart was knocking at her ribs, and she was afraid if she once stopped talking, she'd lose her stride and not utter an intelligent word again.

He was watching her closely now with hooded eyes, his lashes a dark shadow and his lips half parted for words slow to come. "You look like a vision of cotton candy, all dressed in pink."

Feeling an ache in her throat, she swallowed hard and tried to keep the moment light. "You've spent too much time at the fair. Either that, or the sun has baked your brain."

He laughed softly and unceremoniously dumped his ice cubes on her pink-tipped toes. She squealed and jumped up, her feet sliding around in her damp sandals.

His laughter rolled like thunder, warning of deeper emotions. "Serves you right, returning an insult for a compliment. Baked brain, is it?" He dropped the glass and lunged at her.

She kicked off one sandal and used it for defense. But his hands fended off her blows as he caught at her wrists and pulled her quickly against him. Her senses reeling at the sand of his cheek brushing her face, she fought to hold onto her self-control. His eyes were the dark velvet of dusk and she arched away from him, knowing to let him hold her was to invite pain.

Her heart was hammering away like artillery fire as his gaze tangled with hers. He reached out to sift through her hair and trace the curve of her jaw.

"I've missed you, Nat," he admitted, his tone husky.

And she'd missed him, too, but she wasn't going to tell him. Honesty hadn't worked in the past, not nearly so well as holding herself aloof. It had been foolish to come out here and tease him awake. They'd both slipped back into their old friendly relationship. Fun for him perhaps, but dangerous for her.

She stepped away with a light laugh that cost her dearly. "Then it's true—absence does indeed make the heart grow fonder. Quite an admission from a guy who prides himself on watching life from the wings."

For one brief moment, he looked as if she'd slapped him. Maybe it was cruel to jest, to throw back in his face something meant as a confidence. But if he didn't think he was capable of giving love, then he shouldn't set her hopes up, playing at love with husky words and gentle caresses. She was furious with herself, furious with him, too, without quite knowing why.

Turning on one bare heel, she marched toward the back door. The sandal she'd left behind came flying after her. As it landed a foot to her left in a patch of brown grass, she heard him call tauntingly.

"Running away, Nat?"

She might have turned to face him then, might even have weakened and run back to embrace all the risks for one long lingering kiss if he hadn't spoken nastily. As if it was *she* who'd hurt him.

Chapter Eight

The next day Marianne asked Natalie for a completion date for the book, and Natalie made some rough mental calculations. "The rough draft is the hardest part. The revisions will be minor. If all goes well, I could have it ready for the publisher by the first week in September. Do you want me to hurry?"

Marianne twisted the wedding band on her plump finger. "I don't know whether to tell you to hurry up or slow down. It's Harold, you see. I don't need to tell you he hasn't been in favor of the book from the start."

An understanding smile did little to ease Marianne's anxious look. "Yes, I know—though I can't say I understand why he feels as he does."

Marianne heaved herself from the chair and made a turn around the library. "I suppose it's tied up with his concern over the November elections. He wants badly to win, of course, and I think he fears anything discrediting in the book will reflect on him."

"But there isn't anything discrediting *in* the book! Marianne, Jacob Sutton exhibited pioneer ingenuity,

119

initiative, and drive. Those are all fine qualities. Harold should be proud—"

"I know, I know. But he has this fear the book will come out right before elections. Even if it does, I'm sure the likelihood of its attracting any public attention is very remote. I mean, it's a *family* book, with a limited printing."

"I agree, Marianne. It's unlikely the news media would pick up on it, even in the event they realized it was about Harold's ancestors. The last name isn't even the same."

Still, Marianne looked torn with uncertainty.

"If he's that worried, why don't you schedule publication for after the elections?" Natalie said.

"Maybe I'll do that, though I'm anxious to see it in print. I want to *hold* it in my hand!" Marianne said, clutching the invisible book to her heart. Then the cloud of concern returned, and Nat hid a small smile at her worry.

Nat wished her worries could be as simple, but there was nothing simple about Jake Brandon. She'd had no opportunity to speak to him. He couldn't have avoided her more absolutely if she'd been quarantined. At dinner he'd taken little interest in the conversation, had refused to write a press release for Harold, and had even done without a second butterscotch brownie rather than ask her to pass the platter.

If he wanted to be all solemn and sullen, then let him, she thought. She had more important matters on her mind.

Or so she told herself. But that night, as sleep eluded her, her prayers were full of him. What was happening to them, anyway? Why couldn't they simply be friends again? Why did the pain in her heart worsen instead of healing? He'd hurt her, yet when she looked at him, she felt guilty, as if she was somehow responsible for stilling his laughter, for taking away his spirit of fun. He'd even declined Timothy's invitation to the little league game the next night. Now that wasn't like Jake at all!

However, as the next day dawned, there seemed no easy resolution. She threw herself into the task of tying up loose ends in her rough draft. As she did so, Annie Sutton became important again. If Nat was to write short biographies of each of the ten Sutton children, she had to have something more to say about Annie than that she was sensitive to night noises and nearly died of scarlet fever at age ten.

Just as final desperation set in, Hannah knocked at her door, bringing the mail. A letter had come in answer to her ad in a genealogical bulletin for information on David Wayne, the Suttons' family physician.

The writer was a descendant of the doctor and introduced herself as an avid armchair genealogist, but her letter was not all that helpful. The doctor's medical records had been destroyed in an attic fire. She did have, however, the doctor's personal journal.

After debating a while, Nat picked up the phone and dialed the number scribbled at the bottom of the letter. The woman who answered in a creaky old voice, graciously agreed to search Dr. Wayne's journal for some mention of the Sutton family and to call Natalie back. Her return call came in the evening, after the family had gone out, Hannah and Marianne to Timothy's little league game, Harold and Jake to a fundraising dinner where Harold was the speaker.

Natalie quickly jotted down the information about Annie Sutton. Then after thanking the elderly woman for her time and trouble, Nat hung up to mull over the new information.

Dr. Wayne had mentioned Annie Sutton twice in his journal. He had expressed jubilation when Annie recovered from scarlet fever. Then nearly six years later, he'd commented on fearing for her mental well-being.

Figuring Annie to be about sixteen when that last entry was made, Nat chewed on her pencil and tried to imagine Annie's life those long years ago. Being from a wealthy family and having a politically prominent father, she should have been caught up in a whirl of parties and dances and beaus. So what had caused her such mental distress?

Nat picked up her scribbled note and read it again. She'd copied word for word Dr. Wayne's journal entry. She read the last two sentences over again and again:

> Yet emotions run high on the issue of slavery. For the sake of the child, for the sake of all who fear the righteous hand of God, I pray the matter will soon be justly settled.

What matter? Nat wondered. Slavery in general, or something more specific? Yet why would Annie, at age sixteen, be concerning herself to the point of illness over such a grave political and moral issue? Though slaveholding was illegal in Illinois, the government had allowed certain employers to lease slaves from owners in slave territory for marked periods of time. Of course there were those, especially in the southern part of the state, sympathetic with the slaveholders. Did the Sutton family have some connection with slaveholders, some connection that was involved enough to trouble Annie? Considering Jacob Sutton's wealth and social prominence, it was a real possibility. Grabbing a red pencil, Nat underlined the date the entry was written, then unlocked the stairway to the tower.

Compared to the air-conditioned library, it was a furnace. She opened some windows, then searched through the old trunk for the hundredth time for any clues about what had happened in the Sutton family during the spring of 1842.

But there wasn't a single newspaper clipping or personal letter saved from the fall of 1841 to the summer of 1842.

She closed the lid to the trunk and rocked back on her heels. Was there some reason nothing had been saved during that time? Or was it just that nothing noteworthy had happened?

In the oppressive heat of the tower room Nat could not even think clearly. Her blouse was damp with perspiration and clung to her sunburned back and shoulders. The skirt she'd donned just before dinner was wrinkled and smudged with dust and newsprint.

She returned to the library, locked the staircase door, and went upstairs to bathe. The water and the scented bubbles refreshed her but failed to induce any startling insights into Annie.

She slipped into a peppermint-striped sundress, the pink of which matched her sun-flushed cheeks. Two thin straps joined the dress front to back but left her tender shoulders otherwise bare. She fashioned her hair in a loose topknot, leaving sun-streaked tendrils framing her face.

Refreshed and alert once more, she returned to the library to scan local history books for some inkling of events in the Sutton household in the spring of 1842. But she found nothing helpful. Closing the last book and adding it to a tall stack, she let out a weary sigh.

"Something wrong?"

With a swift intake of breath, she looked up to see Jake filling the open doorway of the library. He was an impressive sight in evening dress, and against her will she felt the familiar tug at her heart.

"I can't get anything more concrete than scarlet fever on Annie Sutton, and it's holding up the end-chapter biographies." She watched him work at loosening the collar of his shirt and hated the frailty of her heart that made her want to help him.

"It's as if she dropped off the edge of the earth at sixteen, reappeared a few years later to marry Deane Cruthers, then retreated from the public eye entirely until she died and made the obit column in *The Daily Journal.*"

Jake tossed his tie and evening jacket over a chair back and swept one corner of her desk clean. Perching a lean hip there, he asked, "Annie *who*?"

Her bare feet exploring beneath her desk for the shoes she'd cast off, she found it far easier to be annoyed with him than to fall into the customary strain of their relationship.

"You know Jake, you're sorely lacking in appreciation for your illustrious family tree. Annie Sutton, I said. Oreana Elizabeth. Jacob's only daughter after all those sons. His last child, the little period at the end of the sentence."

He grinned as she paused to catch her breath. "Oreana Elizabeth. You should have said that in the first place. I've never heard her called Annie before."

"It was her childhood nickname. Her brothers called her Annie Softheart Sutton because she was forever adopting orphan pets—a crow with a broken wing, a three-legged dog, and cats by the score. What do you know about her?"

"Less than you, apparently. Why?"

"I don't understand it. At sixteen she should have been the most eligible girl in the county. But according to what little information I have, she was so worried over the issue of slavery she was in danger of a nervous breakdown. Don't you think that's strange?"

"Slavery?" His dark eyebrows shot up. He tapped the stack of books she'd yet to return to the shelves, murmuring evasively, "I don't know, Nat. I've never been a sixteen-year-old girl."

"Then, at eighteen, she married Cruthers, a fortune hunter, and that's the last word on her until her death."

She glared at Jake when he laughed. "What's so funny?"

"You. It's nothing to get worked up over, Nat. All ancient history, anyway. Though I wouldn't advise you to repeat that fortune hunter bit in front of Harold. It would offend his family pride. He covets a family tree ornate with pearls and priceless jewels, even the in-laws. No nuts allowed and certainly nothing as taste-less as a fortune hunter."

She couldn't help smiling a bit. "Where is Harold? I thought the two of you left together."

"We did. Harold's still shaking hands and accepting compliments. Rose is going to drive him home."

"I thought you were home kind of early," she said, then flushed at the admission she'd allowed thoughts of him at all.

"I would have been home sooner, but I stopped by the ballpark in time to see Timothy hit a double. They were winning by a landslide. They're stopping for ice-cream after the game, then going to collect a buddy of

Tim's to stay the night. Mother finally gave in."

He grinned, but he, too, was chatting on a bit nervously. It was hard to believe they'd once been so at ease with one another.

He wandered around the room as she began returning books to the shelves, but his gaze kept coming back to her. His startlingly blue eyes were haunted by reflections she couldn't begin to interpret, and they tripped an uneasy stirring along her nerve endings.

The last book required a stepladder. As she climbed to the second step, she could feel his presence just behind her.

"You're doing it again," he said softly, "reminding me of cotton candy."

Still on the stepladder, she half turned and his eyes took her apart, one feature at a time. He felt her breath catch in her throat as his hands splayed on her slender waist. Throwing caution to the wind, he lifted her down. He did not let her go but stepped closer, inclining his head until his cheek rested against her silky head. He reveled in her sweet fragrance, in the pink glow he'd brought to her cheeks, and the rapid pulse he felt at her temple.

As he brushed her lips with his own, she turned her head. There was a slight tremble in her pleading whisper. "Don't make it any harder than it is, Jake. It wouldn't mean anything anyway."

"Who says it wouldn't?" he whispered against her lips.

"*You* said it. Maybe not in so many words, but you said it."

"Then forget what I said." He caught her chin and stroked fresh color to her cheeks with a compliment.

"You know, Nat, you grow prettier every day. Why is that, I wonder?"

"I don't! I've always been plain."

"Who told you that? You aren't the least bit plain. You've a smile angels would envy, hair as soft and fine as a baby's, and dreamy faraway eyes that defy description." He watched her lower her dark lashes and gave a throaty chuckle. "Am I embarrassing you?"

"No," she said, but her gaze lifted no higher than the startling white of his shirt front. "Now, if you're quite through…"

"But I'm not. I was just warming up." His hands folded around the firm flesh of her upper arms lest she try to elude him. Adopting a hushed tone, he said, "You've also got a smashing figure, slender, but smashing. And the cutest little derr—"

Natalie clapped a hand over his mouth and sputtered, "That's enough, Jake Brandon! Not another word!"

He kissed the palm of her hand, and when she drew it away as if she'd been bitten, he laughed. "Come for a walk with me, Nat."

"No."

"Oh, come on. If I promise to behave myself?"

"No!"

Knowing it was a delaying tactic, he fished in his pocket and came out with a butterscotch. "I don't know if I can explain it, Nat. But somewhere between my third and fifth yawn—Harold's policies are sound, but his speeches are a dead bore—everything fell into place.

"You've been right about a couple of things, and I'm in your debt. 'I'm sorry' truly is a healing statement. It's worked wonders with Harold. If I say it to you, can

I expect the same miracle?"

She didn't answer for a long moment, and he entreated her forgiveness with a tender, beseeching look.

"Sorry for what?" she asked at last.

"Sorry for being such a self-contained jerk, for trying to stay uninvolved, for discouraging you when you so sweetly confessed your love."

"I don't want to talk about that," she said in a low whisper.

"Then we won't. Come for a walk, and I'll tell you what's wrong with your book. Would you like that?"

Looking at him then, she accused, "Then it *was* you who leafed through it while I was gone."

He hooked an arm through hers and led her toward the door. "Yes, I admit it. I'm a snoop. I don't respect other people's privacy, I can't keep secrets, and I've been known to correct misspelled words. And those are my good qualities. Your spelling, by the way, is atrocious."

"That isn't fair. It's a rough draft. If you wanted to read my manuscript, you should have been polite enough to ask."

He showed little remorse. "Where's your compassion, Nat? I was knocking around the house, all out of sorts, missing you. Hannah'd put fresh flowers in your room and left your door standing open."

His hand tightening on her elbow, he admitted, "It wasn't the flowers that lured me in, though. It was your perfume. I found myself wondering if your fragrance really did hang in the air or if my mind was so full of you I merely imagined it. So I stepped in. What is that perfume you wear, anyway?" he asked, pausing at the front door to lean near.

His mustache tickled the underside of her ear, and

she teetered on the edge of uncertainty, torn between pushing him away and pulling him closer, losing herself in the kiss she knew he would give with the slightest encouragement. But she had tasted the ashes of rejection, and caution won out. He was too carefree and capricious.

She planted the heel of her hand against his shirt front and spoke in an almost steady voice. "You said you'd behave, yet we aren't even out the door and you're giving me reason to doubt you. I don't think I need a walk tonight. In fact, I think I'll go upstairs and clean the ink off my typewriter keys."

"How adventuresome! Of course, if you give in to tidiness, you'll never know the flaw I found in your manuscript."

"I'm not all that worried."

He chuckled and swung open the door, then with an exaggerated gesture, indicated there was plenty of room for her to pass through without risking contact with him. One step into the open doorway, she stopped to glare at his mockery. A moth gave up beating at the glass chimney of a veranda light and stirred her hair in passing.

"Hurry up, you're letting bugs in. Hannah'll have your hide tacked to flypaper," he warned.

She stepped out on the veranda just as twin headlights came up the lane and pinned her in their glare. Squinting, she lifted her hand. The lights and motor went off, car doors flew open, and Timothy, in dusty jeans and a baseball shirt emblazoned with his team's name, hopped up the veranda steps dragging a suitcase and a fellow ballplayer.

"Boy, did we cream them!" he bragged, swaggering a bit as he advanced on Natalie and Jake.

"Jake told me your team was winning," Natalie said. "Congratulations."

"Did he tell you I got a double? It was a good one, wasn't it, Uncle Jake?"

"It sure was." Jake ruffled his hair, then reminded, "Don't you think you'd better introduce us to your friend?"

"Oh, sure! This is Kenny. Kenny, meet my Uncle Jake and Natalie. Natalie's a writer. We can't bother her when she's writing. But the rest of the time, she's okay."

The boy who'd been hanging back stepped forward and grinned. With a cowlick three inches tall, a bruised cheek, and scraped knuckles, Kenny looked as if he spoke mischief fluently.

"Hello, Kenny. Tim's been looking forward to your coming for a long time. I'm sure the two of you are going to have lots of fun."

"No, we're not, Nat," Timothy said hastily. "I promised Grandma Marianne we'd be good."

"Angels," Kenny added, making himself a halo with a circling finger.

Hannah passed them on the steps, making a low growl in her throat. Jake smothered a laugh, and Marianne shooed the boys toward the front door. They went along, Timothy listing all the things they *weren't* allowed to do.

"Would you please park the car in the garage, Jake? I want to make sure Timothy takes a bath," Marianne called back.

"I'll put it away later. Nat and I were just about to take a walk."

"Later's fine," she said and closed the door behind her.

Jake sauntered down the steps, then turned to wait for Natalie. "Aren't you coming?"

"I think I've been maneuvered," she grumbled, just for appearance's sake, for she really did want to walk with him.

The lawn was cracked and dry; the grass whispered beneath their feet as they walked. Crickets and fireflies lent soothing touches, and Nat caught the scent of roses as they passed a garden trellis. She eased out a long sigh as peace settled in.

When Jake took her hand, she stilled her quickening heart. He was a man given to touching, lightly, without meaning. She'd learned that the hard way.

They passed a field made mysterious by darkness. An occasional dagger of heat lightning pierced the sky. They had only that and a pale moon to guide their steps, yet Jake walked with a steady surefootedness. Nat knew without asking where he was leading. The deer park always seemed to draw him.

He squeezed her hand, and she smiled. "See?" he said. "You're revived already. You needed the fresh air. I needed the company. We're both cured."

"You get lonely?" she blurted and could have swallowed her tongue.

"I never used to feel lonely," he said. "But lately, it's crept up on me with disturbing frequency. Sometimes I feel lonely in a room full of people. Sometimes, in a room with just one person, a person who won't get her nose out of a history book or her fingers off the typewriter keys, I get the loneliest feeling of all."

In a flash of heat lightning, she searched his face, expecting laughter to shine from his eyes. But there was no laughter there. Confused and uncertain, she fell back on a safer topic.

She freed her hand from his, making a grand production of shaking a pebble out of her shoe. "You were going to tell me the flaw in my manuscript. Be gentle, though. I have a tender ego."

"You're a good writer, Nat. I only intended to read the first paragraph or two, but soon I was turning pages. I was hooked!"

"Then you like it?"

He did not answer immediately, searching instead for just the right words. Nat couldn't stand the silence.

"You didn't like it," she said in a flat voice.

"Let's just say I'm having a little trouble getting it labeled. It isn't fiction, but it doesn't seem quite history either."

"But it is history," she insisted. "I was very careful with the research. I've read through that whole trunk of material in the tower room and scanned all the county history books in your library."

"It isn't your research I'm finding fault with. It's your conjectures. You have a flowing style that fleshes out old Jacob, gives him a personality, likes and dislikes, passions and promises. He practically steps off the page."

"But that's good! Isn't it?"

"If you're writing fiction, it's great. But this is supposed to be history, Nat. The man's dead and buried. All you're expected to do is list his accomplishments."

"But that's boring!"

"Maybe, to some people. But you can't know what sort of man Jacob Sutton was unless you lived back then and knew him intimately."

"But certain conclusions can be drawn. If he hadn't been ambitious, hardworking, determined, he never would have succeeded."

"I'll go along with you that far. But you don't know he was compassionate, warm, a good father and husband and friend. Nat, the man you've depicted ought to be nominated for sainthood!"

Defensive and just beginning to be aware how important it was to her that he *like* the book, she said peevishly, "Well, that's how I view him. Isn't that what history is all about? One man stands out, captures the imagination—"

"Maybe I'm wrong. But it seems to me you've taken the liberty to fashion him into the man you'd like to think he was."

At the last moment, she silenced the rebuttal trembling on her lips. What he said could be more true than false. Another volley of lightning lit the sky, and as she picked Jake's face out of the darkness, it became suddenly clear to her what she had done. She'd painted old Jacob as the man she saw in Jake, a man of character, honesty, compassion, and humor.

As they approached the fence closing off the deer park, she spoke softly. "You could be right, Jake. But your mother seems pleased with the book as it is, and after all, I did draw my conjectures from my research." *Or most of them anyway*, she thought lamely, linking her fingers through the wires of the fence. "There isn't anyone of Jacob's era alive to contradict me. And if I've made mistakes, they're honest ones. If I were to write it over, I don't know how I'd do it any differently."

"Then maybe you shouldn't write it at all."

"Not write it?" she cried. "Don't be silly. I have to! I've been commissioned to write it—I want to write it. It's important to me. Someday, Jake, I want to be taken seriously as a writer. I'm willing to work hard, and somehow this seems like my first really big step in the right direction. I'm proud of being asked to do this book for your family, and I want to be proud when it's done."

"I understand that, Nat."

"Then why would you suggest that I give up now? That I not write it at all?"

"Because I don't ever want you to be ashamed of it someday down the road."

"Why would I be?"

Gazing over the grassy enclosure where trees stood dark and silent, he ignored her question. "There's a doe. See there?"

"Why would I be ashamed, Jake? You can't say something like that and just leave it hanging."

"Yes I can," he said mildly. He refused to discuss the book any further, choosing instead to lounge against a fence post and watch what was, in his own mind anyway, a deer.

She felt disgruntled. "It's probably a dead tree stump."

"No it isn't. It's a deer. I think there's a fawn, too."

"Pooh. You can't see any better than I can. It's too dark."

"Keeping them in captivity ruins their instincts," he said, unruffled. "But Mother loves them. Over the years, she's had some so tame they'd eat from her hand."

"At least they're safe."

"Safe? I suppose. But it's an unrealistic existence. Maybe a little chance would be more satisfying."

She heard the quizzical quality of his voice and wondered at it, thought it was an odd statement coming from a man who'd a short time ago claimed he watched life from the wings. If he expected an argument from her, he wasn't going to get it. He was right. Getting involved with people, loving—it was risky.

"What do you want from life, Nat?" he asked suddenly.

She could feel him watching her closely but felt concealed by the darkness and her own directions.

"Just what I said. To be a really good writer. I'd like to be a better person, too, I guess, but everybody says that. And maybe I'd like to make pots and pots of money."

He gave a shout of laughter that put the doe—it wasn't a tree stump after all—to flight. "Everyone says that, too!" he pointed out.

"If you're enjoying yourself, go ahead and have your laugh. But someday you'll come begging for my autograph." She tilted her head and gave what she hoped to be an aristocratic sniff.

"You'll make me beg, after all we've meant to each other? Hard woman, you." His tone had grown husky. His hands found hers and held them firmly.

In the darkness he was a tall form anchored near enough to trigger responses that played on one another like dominoes: rapid pulse, mushrooming heart, and a catch in her throat. Her words came out breathlessly. "I might reconsider, and if you ask nicely, toss the autograph in with the book at no extra charge."

His hands slid up her arms in a caressing motion. "You'll never make it, you know, if you insist on seeing only the bright side of life. Even children's fairy tales aren't all sunshine and clover. That bit of suffering along the way makes the joys that much richer."

"I know that!"

"Then you shouldn't mind my reminding you."

She shook his hands off her arms and stood back where he would not guess his touch made her tremble inside. Indignation fired her voice. "You know, this conversation is all backwards! *I'm* the one who told *you* life is to be lived, not watched. *I'm* the one who said caring about others is the right way to live. *I'm* the one who advocated loving even when it hurts!"

"You make such a good case. How is it you failed to convince me?" he asked, his hands lighting on her sunburned shoulders, pressing into flesh made tender by too much sun.

As she tried to wriggle free, his hold strengthened until she winced and cried out. "Jake, let go! That hurts."

Instantly, he released her. "Your sunburn, I forgot."

But the pain didn't stop, for it was more on the inside than out. Quick tears stung her eyes. Not long ago, he'd told her not to ask for more than he could give. Now he was asking for more than she could give, for she was not going to be held and kissed and caressed by a man who could not or would not love her.

She moved down the fence, her back to him, but was aware that he followed, for the woodsy, pungent male scent that reminded her of a pine forest in winter stayed with her.

"Nat, stop a minute," he implored. "I'm saying this very badly for a man who makes his living with words. What I've been trying to tell you is that I realized something this evening as Harold droned on and on. Something important. Something you'd already tried to tell me. You can buy life insurance, but you can't buy relationship insurance. Maybe that's what I've been wanting all along—a guarantee that if I give in to my feelings for you it won't end up badly.

"Nat?" He reached out for her elbow and turned her to face him, careful not to touch her shoulders. "What I'm trying to say is I love you. I guess I started falling in love with you that first day when you were frantically searching for a place to hide the evidence you'd spilled coffee on one of Mother's sacred antiques.

"You leave sunshine on everything you touch, Nat, and that's a precious gift. You've thawed out old Hannah, you've befriended Tim, and you've helped me mend ties with Harold. You may not say much about your faith, but you live it.

"I thought I had a handle on love once, but it slipped away. My marriage to Gina was built on shallow dreams that couldn't endure. I made changes in my life then. I tried to let God run things. And just when I thought things might work out, Gina was killed."

Seeing his heart twist with pain, she reached out to touch his face, to smooth the fine lines bracketing his eyes, to brush a tumble of curls back from his high brow.

"Jake, I'm so sorry," she said when she could trust her voice not to crack with her emotion.

"Me, too. Because she was young. Because I never shared love with her as God intended. Because she carried my child."

"She carried your child?" How that must have hurt! Unable to look into his eyes for fear the hurt was still etched there, Nat hid her face in his shirt and whispered, "I didn't know."

Jake held her close, comforting when it was she who should be comforting him. "I always felt I failed Gina. And when it was all over, I promised myself I wouldn't fail anyone else."

As he rocked her gently, his chin resting on her head, she understood why he'd fought not to love, why he'd convinced himself it hurt less not to care at all. But his caring was everywhere. His family, Hannah, even in the subject matter of his written pieces. In his behavior, he'd always known faith without love was empty.

"I tell you all this because I want you to understand I'm not like your invented Jacob. I'm not Superman by a far cry. But I love you, and I'd give a butterscotch moon to hear you say it just one more time.

"Say what, Jake?"

"That you love me."

She rose on her tiptoes and, heart singing for joy, said against his mouth, "I love you for free. You can keep your butterscotch moon."

In the glitter of lightning, she saw his last anxiety fall away and his lips curve into a smile so joyful her knotted fear of rejection liquefied and flowed away as if it had never been.

A feather-light kiss brushed her pulsing temple, beginning a trail that paused at the delicate shell of her ear. Whispered endearments stirred her, and when his lips met hers in a kiss both tender and careful, she met it with such passion his reserve was shattered. His kisses became a branding fire, spreading pleasure and wonder to the very tips of her frosted toenails. She strained nearer, and her fingers wound their way through hair dark as the night, curls that had long tempted her touch.

A novice at love, she nonetheless sensed the fine line beyond which caution was carelessly thrown to the wind, and as his clean-shaven jaw brushed her sunburn, his lips teasing the throbbing pulse at her throat, she said with a silvery shiver, "We'd better start back."

He traced the shape of her lips with a blunt-tipped finger, then kissed away the tingling wake of his touch. As his kisses deepened and she felt her common sense sailing away with the moon, she whispered with more urgency. "Jake!"

He let her widen the distance between them then, protesting only with a low, wry sound in his throat. "I suppose you're right," he murmured.

Their walk back would not have won any medals in speed. Their arms wound around one another, frequently stopping for stolen kisses and warm caresses, they gave no thought to the measure of time. There were only the two of them, the misty moon, and God in heaven to witness their love.

Chapter Nine

The howling wind slung rain against the house in whooshing, gusting sheets. Awakened from a sound but brief sleep, Natalie hugged the sheet up under her chin. A gentle, soaking rain would have been nice, but after the hot dry weather, rain of any kind was welcome.

With an inward smile, she recalled how as a child she'd shivered under the covers when the thunder shouted and the lightning sent electric fingers across the sky. Somewhere along the line she'd lost her fear and now found storms rather exhilarating from the cozy comfort of a warm bed. There was no need to fear storms of nature or of life when the peace of God reigned in her heart.

Thoroughly awake, she listened a while. Then as the wind slackened, she closed her eyes, thinking of Jake and thanking God for the bright and beautiful gift of his love. She was glad to be awake, the edge of her weariness gone so she could savor the golden warmth of his confession. Her heart was full of joy and she held her pillow tight, just as Jake had held her.

How silly she'd been to fear falling in love, to consider a commitment to a man a grave threat to her career! As she basked in a glowing loveshine, she saw that giving was always the victor over taking. When she gave love to a friend, to a child, to that one very special man, her love was multiplied and sent back in ways that could not be numbered. That was God's mystery of love.

She hugged her pillow happily. Jake's love had already enriched her life with the spiritual joy he touched within, with the physical wonder of his lips awakening desires she'd never guessed she possessed, with his endearing understanding of her shyness about those desires.

Knowing her dream, he would never threaten it in any way. Even her writing would benefit from Jake's love. As he broadened her world, her love would deepen her writing.

Thinking of her writing reminded her she'd left her manuscript, notes, and papers strewn all over the desk in the library. Harold would be using the library in the morning, and she always kept her materials out of his way. Unlike Jake, Harold had a fetish for neatness. He'd find the disorganized desk annoying.

So thinking, Nat glanced at the clock on her night-stand. One o'clock. Maybe she'd better slip downstairs and tidy up a bit. Not bothering with slippers, she tied on her robe and opened the door to her room.

Glad to see a light had been left on downstairs, she descended soundlessly, the silkiness of her robe cool against her legs. Angling off toward the library, she stopped short. A broad shaft of light shone out the door into the parlor. She could hear the low rumble of voices—Harold's and Jake's.

Hesitant over barging in on what must be a private discussion to be conducted at such an odd hour, Nat prepared to return the way she'd come. However a certain indefinable quality in Jake's voice arrested her attention, and she paused, listening guiltily.

"That's all? You got me out of bed in the middle of the night to show me this scribbled scrap of paper?"

Harold cursed under his breath and uttered a tense command. "Read it, would you?"

"I already did."

"It's Natalie's handwriting, isn't it?"

"Without a doubt. But I still don't see it's such great cause for alarm. I've told you all along she's sharp."

Somehow, it seemed less than a compliment. Feeling a prickle of unease, she edged closer, unwilling to miss a word. She was eaten up with curiosity to know what scribbled scrap they'd found and why on earth Harold was upset and Jake defensive.

"And *I* told Mother there'd be complications, but she wouldn't listen," Harold said. "She assured me there wasn't one speck of incriminating evidence in that trunk or this library."

When Jake made no response, Harold demanded in a distrustful tone, "I want to know how she got a line on this."

"Then maybe you should ask her."

"So help me, if I find out you told her—"

"I promised I wouldn't and I didn't. Now if you're through with this interrogation, I'm going back to bed."

Heart pounding, knowing she couldn't leave the parlor without being seen, she backed into the shadows. But Harold stopped Jake before he made it out the door.

"I'm *not* finished. Look, Jake, if it seems I'm accusing you, just remember you've never given me much reason to think you'd work in my interest."

"I thought we'd talked that out, wiped the slate clean."

"Maybe we wiped it a bit hastily. I've got enough to worry about with my political opponent, I shouldn't have to worry about bad press coming out of my own house."

"I've never given you bad press."

"I wasn't referring to you."

"Natalie isn't press, so why don't you leave her out of it?"

"How can I? She's the whole problem!"

"No, she isn't. Mother's the one who wants the book."

"True. But Natalie's just another hungry writer! If she catches a whiff of scandal, she'll build it up for all it's worth, just for the byline. Politicians are always fair game but never more so than in an election year."

"It's been one hundred fifty years, Harold. Even if she does get a line on it, what difference can it make?"

"What difference? I can't believe you're that ignorant! 'Senatorial Hopeful, Great-Great-Great-Grandson of—' "

"Again, so what?" Jake interrupted. "You aren't to blame. What can anyone make of it?"

"You obviously don't understand the subtle art of mudslinging. All it takes is a suggestion planted in an undecided mind, and bingo, you lose a vote!"

"A vote or two..."

"I'm the underdog! I can't afford a vote or two! Here's what I want you to do, Jake."

"Not me, fella. I'm not doing anything."

"You keep her quiet! I mean it!" Harold boomed so loud Nat's heart missed a full beat. "She obviously fancies herself madly in love with you. Now you'd better make it pay off. Keep track of her, find out what she's up to, and if she even *looks* like she's going anywhere near the press, you'd better shut her up. I don't care how you do it—promise her you'll marry her, if that's what it takes—but keep her quiet."

"You're positively paranoid," Jake said in disgust. "I'm telling you, it wouldn't make a bit of difference if you were John Wilkes Booth's great-great-great-grandson...."

"I might be better off if I were!"

Natalie had heard enough to confuse her for a decade or two. She didn't want to listen to that hauteur-edged voice lash out at Jake any longer, for it was as if with each crack of the verbal whip, Harold peeled away the joy that had enveloped her.

Keeping to the shadows, she crept out of the parlor, up the stairs, and back to bed. The lightning and thunder had stopped and the rain had gentled, yet she shivered from sheer nerves.

Jake loves me, she told herself again and again. His eyes had beamed messages of love to her very soul; his arms had held her as if he would never let her go; his kisses had not lied.

If Harold's words hadn't taken away the certainty of Jake's love, they had at least tarnished it. No matter how much she assured herself Jake had not pretended his love down at the deer park, Harold had planted a weedy doubt. She shivered again.

But, no! She continued the circling battle. Jake was too honest to lie with words and actions. She wasn't going to let Harold's tirade fill her with disquieting "supposes."

What exactly was behind Harold's tirade anyway? His strong feelings against the book, of course. But something more, too.

As Jake had said, she wasn't a press person. Why would she go to the press? And with what? Why did Harold fear she was about to discover something so unpleasant she could use it to make him lose the election. And why would Harold think she'd enjoy crippling his chances of winning? Jake was right! He *was* paranoid.

Now think! she commanded her brain. What was she missing? The scribbled note that had set Harold off. It would have to be the information she'd taken over the phone, the excerpt from Dr. Wayne's journal about Annie's fragile mental state. Her frown deepened. The stray thought that wiggled to the front of her mind had been lurking in the background all evening.

Could it be that Jacob Sutton not only sympathized with slaveholders but that he was a slaveholder himself? Could he have used slave labor in his saltworks? She found the thought not at all to her liking. For one thing, it smacked of northern hypocrisy. For another, Jacob, who'd been so gentle with his daughter, surely could not have so callously abused people of another skin color.

However, she had to investigate. Something else Harold had said disturbed her deeply—Marianne must

146

have held back pieces of family information. She had, on several occasions, discouraged Nat from going to the county genealogical files and the county court-house.

Maybe it was time Nat put more than one Brandon to the test. She mapped out a plan, then drifted in and out of sleep until daylight.

It was still raining. Nat dressed in jeans, a plaid cotton shirt, and tennis shoes. With neither the time nor the patience to tame her hair, she pulled it back in a ponytail, knotted a scarf around it, and went down to breakfast.

Timothy and his pal Kenny were just finishing up. Harold was glumly worrying a cup of coffee, and Jake—heart-jolting Jake—rose from the table with a brilliant smile and kissed her in front of one and all.

Coloring but determined to have this over, to still the doubting Thomas in her, she smiled in Hannah's direction.

"Nothing for me but a glass of juice, Hannah. I'm in a hurry to be off."

Cup halfway to his mouth, Harold feigned nonchalance. "Oh? Where might you be off to so bright and early?"

She waited until he took a sip to respond in equally casual tones. "To the office of *The Daily Journal*. Why? Would you like to go along?"

Harold choked and spewed coffee. As he reached for a napkin, his eyes sought out Jake's, a wild warning in them. When he had control of his breath again, he said, "I've a full morning. Jake would no doubt be pleased to accompany you, though."

She turned to him with a chipper invitation in her

green eyes. "How about it, Jake? Would you like to ride along?" she asked, careful not to betray by even the swift flick of an eyelash how much weighed in the balance.

"I don't think so, Nat," he said as he jellied a slice of toast and gave Harold one long meaningful smile. "I told the boys I'd run them over to the roller rink if it continues to rain. There isn't much for them to do, shut up indoors."

Nat gave him one last shot. "We could all go together. We could drop the boys at the roller rink, then go on to the newspaper office."

Relief without measure flooded over her as he shook his dark tumble of curls and cracked a grin. "No offense, Nat, but I'd rather skate than hang around *The Daily Journal*. But wait a second. I'll walk you out to your car."

"What? And get all wet?" she asked, suddenly very frightened again. Would he try to talk her out of going? Try to find out what she was up to?

But he only dashed beside her through the rain to the garage, laughing as he shook the rain out of his hair and rubbed a wet nose to hers. "Drive carefully. The rain has slickened the roads. If you want to, stop and skate with us a while. We could all go for hamburgers, too."

"That sounds like fun," she agreed. "If I finish at the newspaper office, I'll join you."

Again, she caught her breath, fearing he'd ask what she was bent on finishing, but he didn't. Rather, he tipped up her face and ran a finger down the length of her cheek, disturbing a beading of raindrops. A frown knit his brow.

"You look tired. Didn't you sleep well?"

"Not very," she confessed, thrilling to the touch of his fingers roaming her face.

"Any special reason?" He dipped nearer to ask.

She let a giggle explain.

"I hoped as much," he said with a crooked grin. Then he lowered his mouth, making a leisurely picnic of a kiss and setting off a wild tumult within her.

The scent of rain on his skin, the taste of it on his lips, the warmth of him standing so close, the sound of his voice making a husky caress of her name—all her senses were invigorated by him. Linking her hands around his neck, she tilted her head back and emptied her soul in a smile.

In that moment, it seemed impossible she could have doubted his sincerity. "I love you, Jake Brandon."

"I always did think you were bright." He kissed tendrils of hair gone to curl in the damp air.

"What an ego. No one warned me."

"No one warned me about you either—that you'd make me think of violets and rainbows, that I'd feel like half a person when you're gone for a couple of days, that you'd knock me breathless with a kiss."

He had touched her lips again when she remembered the mission ahead of her and stepped away with a shaky laugh.

"I really should get going now."

"What? When we're having such a splendid time saying good-bye?"

His freshly shaven cheek was smooth and cool against hers, his last hug infinitely tender. As he helped her into her car he said, "Hamburgers at noon. Don't forget. And this evening, we'll go somewhere nice, just the two of us. We have a lot of catching up to do."

"Catching up?"

"For all the time I felt like gathering you close and kissing you senseless and didn't." He touched her face one last time, then stepped away so she could back out her car.

Her heart did a happy hum to the tune of the windshield wipers. Her fingers never touched the radio dial, yet her soul bubbled with music all the way to the office of *The Daily Journal*.

There, the music stopped.

The Daily Journal had begun publication in 1835, and every copy was stored on microfilm. It took Natalie only part of a morning to discover the truth Harold—and yes, Marianne, too—had hidden.

Jacob Sutton had indeed leased slaves to work in his salt wells and furnaces. That wasn't, however, the end of the bad news. He had been charged and tried in the spring of 1842 for illegal trafficking in slaves.

The accusations were grim. He was said to have been involved in catching runaways as they crossed onto the free soil of Illinois and returning them to their owners for a tidy profit. In some cases, the paper reported, he had even destroyed freedom papers and sold free people back into slavery.

Nat kept a tight lock on her emotions, determined to read through the entire account of the trial before she gave in and was heartsick. *Jacob is innocent until proved guilty,* she kept reminding herself.

Jacob Sutton was acquitted.

She might, she thought as she passed the roller rink without even slowing, allow herself to feel a measure of relief. A judge and jury had found the man innocent. Was it cynical of her to wonder if the ruling was true and just or if the decision was swayed by influence?

The persistence of the rain and the gray clouds that scudded along in a watery sky mirrored Natalie's spirits as she drove home. She felt keen disappointment on one level, disappointment over the man Jacob Sutton *might* have been. On a far more private plane, she was anguished. *Jake!* her heart cried, but she stifled the sound and gripped the steering wheel hard, refusing to think of his part in the deception yet.

Far safer to hold thoughts of Jake at bay, to deal with old Jacob Sutton first. She thought with an embarrassment approaching humiliation of the portrait of a fine man she'd painted in strong, glowing words. Under her pen, he'd become a demigod, a summation of every good quality any man could possess, a man of keen intelligence, ambition, insight, and sound business technique.

Hogwash and baloney? Had she been wrong about old Jacob through and through? Just last night, Jake had tried to say...No! not yet. She couldn't deal with that yet.

The house was empty and silent. She found a note in the kitchen, directing the hungry to a platter of sandwiches in the refrigerator. Hannah and Marianne had gone to a luncheon, and Harold was off at some rain-soaked county fair pumping hands.

She ate a sandwich automatically, hardly tasting it. She drank a glass of milk, then went to the library, collected her manuscript and the scrap of paper that had set off Harold's tirade, and went up to her room.

In blind desperation she scanned the manuscript, her conviction growing. The book couldn't go to the press. Had there been a fireplace in her room, she would have cast the manuscript in and watched it burn. It seemed worthless. "Hire Natalie Franklin. She writes history the way it should have been!" she hissed with a sarcasm foreign to her nature.

As she paced her room, her anger grew. Anger with Marianne for not being honest with her, anger with Harold for being too concerned with his political chances to care about an eager young writer's devastating error. Anger with Jake. Most of all, anger with Jake! He'd known and he hadn't told her. That was the promise he'd made to Harold, the promise he'd kept, even at the expense of their relationship. For she'd told him her dream. And he understood the importance of truth in the written word. Or at least, she thought he did. Had she been wrong about that, too? Wrong about Jake, just as she had been about Jacob Sutton?

Innocent until proved guilty. Who was innocent? Jacob Sutton or Jake? No, not Jake. He hadn't been honest with her. Even if old Jacob was entirely innocent, someone should have told her about that trial. Someone should have told her what poor Annie went through.

She stopped short on that thought. She had no foundation for assuming that Annie's anguish had been caused by the humiliation of seeing her father's name dragged through the mud.

The confusing, interplaying thoughts were coming too fast and furiously. She desperately needed to clear her brain. Grabbing a hooded rain jacket from her closet, she dashed down the stairs and out the front door to collide headlong into Jake.

She sucked in her breath as he reached out to steady her, his strong touch melting through her jacket and shirt, his eyes dancing with surprised laughter, his errant curls glistening with rain.

"So here's the woman who stood us up, running out on us again," he said to his small companions.

"What happened to you, Nat?" Timothy demanded. "I wanted to show you how good I can skate."

"I'm sorry, Tim. I got tied up," she said past a lump in her throat, eaten up with humiliation. How could a man who had betrayed her still weaken her?

Blinded by unbidden tears, she dashed on down the steps, ignoring Jake's shouted "Hey, where are you off to now?"

Afraid he might try to catch up with her, she jumped into her car, drove a little way down the lane, then shut off the motor and climbed out.

Crossing the fence into the timbered area of the deer park proved a challenge, for her tomboy days were long past. But her feet finally settled on the spongy layers of dead leaves, and the rain, which had turned misty and gentle, was no problem beneath the shelter of huge trees. A splat here, a drip there, she thought, wiping her face and likening the widespread green branches to a rather old and reliable umbrella.

Thigh-high, thickly matted undergrowth soaked her jeans, and the dampness of the ground eventually leaked into her tennis shoes. But she was mindless of the discomfort, her mind busily fitting odd-shaped pieces together to fill in the puzzle.

She could assume from Harold's desperation to keep

the trial hidden that old Jacob was guilty. Jake surely felt he was guilty, too. Why else would he bear his ancestor's name more like a burden than a privilege?

And he had not told her. His opportunities had been limitless. Why, just last night he had suggested her slant on old Jacob might be incorrect.

But that was as close as he'd come to being honest with her, to sparing her the humiliation of seeing the book go to press as it was written, and becoming the laughingstock of the historical community. For certainly all the serious historians in the area knew about old Jacob's trial. That was why Marianne had hired someone out of the area! And why she'd wanted to limit the research to only her own painstakingly compiled research material.

Sidestepping a patch of poison ivy and a tangle of old berry bushes, she found a wet stump and plopped down. What a mindless trusting moron she'd been! Not even the rankest amateur reporter would let previously compiled material stand as the sole resources for a written piece.

But then, came a small voice of defense, Nat had never claimed to be a reporter. Fiction had always been her first love.

Cheered by the rain after the long dry spell, the birds went about their usual business, flitting from tree branch to tree branch, a wren calling, a woodpecker knocking for lunch.

She heaved out a sigh, thinking, *Life goes on.* Time to face the big question. Had Jake ever really loved her? Or was he just two jumps ahead of Harold, keeping track of her movements in a much more subtle and unforgivable way? She had loved him, trusted him, and all the time he'd been hiding crucial information for the book she'd been commissioned to write. Her first big break.

Good word, *break.*

Her mind made up, she returned to the house.

Chapter Ten

Hoping to buy some time before anyone discovered she'd returned, she parked the car in the garage and entered the house soundlessly, muddy shoes in hand.

From the direction of the kitchen, she could hear Jake's voice over the lilt of little boy voices. "Okay, fellas, let's clean up this mess. Then you two are going to have to entertain yourselves for a while. I promised Harold I'd smooth out his speech for tomorrow night. Come on, get cracking."

The deep timbre of his voice pummeled her heart. She climbed the stairs on fresh waves of pain, knowing her decision was right. She had to get out of here because the tears would not stay at bay forever. And she wanted no witnesses to her crashing defeat.

In her room, she dropped her wet clothes in a pile and slipped into lavender slacks and a lavender and white striped polo shirt. Her hair, just curly enough to be uncooperative in humid weather, stubbornly persisted in floating about her face like a warm honey-brown cloud.

She turned away from a mirror that declared her green eyes too large and empty for her white face and

157

systematically began to pack.

One matter remained. She could not just go. Marianne had hired her and deserved an explanation. Despite her resentment of Marianne's subterfuge, Nat was fond of the woman. Nor could she go without saying good-bye to Timothy and Hannah. *And Jake?* came a whispering she chose to ignore.

Her bags packed, her books in boxes, her typewriter in the case waiting to be carried out to the car, she grew restless for Hannah and Marianne to return.

She opened her door and listened. Soft music flowed from Jake's room. He was working. Assured she wouldn't run into him, she descended the stairs and found Tim and Kenny arm-wrestling in front of the television.

Tim, decidedly the loser and ungraciously so, declared, "I wish we could go outside. There's nothing to do in here but stupid arm wrestling."

Nat worked the station selector and found an old jungle movie that satisfied the pair temporarily.

Her nerves were jumping as the wait became increasingly hard. She took another sandwich and a bottle of soda from the refrigerator, then climbed up to the tower room.

Half an hour of watching the misty rainfall had her more unsettled than ever, so unsettled she was now imagining sounds in the stairway. She was eerily reminded of Annie and her diary entry about night noises. But this was broad daylight, and she was a grown woman—a silly fanciful woman. At the merest scraping of metal on metal, she turned briskly about and crossed the tower room to the landing.

She listened hard above the empty stairway. At first all she heard was the pounding of her own heart. *Ri-*

diculous, she scolded herself, wiping moist hands down the legs of her slacks. She continued to listen. The sound came as a whisper, then louder, hoarser, almost urgent.

She faced the door across the landing from the tower room and knew with a certainty someone was behind it. Laying no claim to bravery, she was about to fly down the stairs when the door jerked open and two impish faces popped out, gasped, then retreated.

"Timothy Brandon, you little stinker, come back here!" The scare he'd given her sharpened her voice.

By the time one sheepish face reappeared, she was beginning to see the humor in the situation. Two bored little boys had gone looking for adventure, and she, with her imagination running rampant, had been primed to overreact. She spoke again, less sharply this time. "What do you two think you're doing?"

Kenny, who gave the impression he wouldn't flinch at Godzilla himself, had eyes as big as pie plates. He stammered, "I-it's awful d-dark in there."

"We were just looking around," said Tim, looking guilty but not too alarmed.

"At what?"

"Nothing," they chimed, locking their eyes on their shoes.

"You must have been looking at something," Nat persisted, knowing better than to let them off too easily.

"Well, Kenny said some of the old men in town told him they used to keep slaves up here. I told him that was stupid, but he said to prove it, so we came up to have a look." Tim shifted from one foot to the other, daring to glance at her for a reaction.

159

"All right. Now you've had your look. Go back down."

Shamefaced, they both started down the stairs, neither one suspecting Tim's innocent words had caught her in a stranglehold. A clank on the stairs, another glance from guilty eyes, and Nat saw how they'd gotten in. She held out her hand.

"Give me the key, Tim."

Reluctant to hand it over, he said, "I'll put it back where I found it, I promise, Nat. You won't tell on me, will you?"

That would hardly be fair since she planned to enter the forbidden room herself. "The key, Tim," she said more gently.

He sighed in defeat, then tossed it up to her, grumbling to Kenny, "Boy, I'll bet I'm in for it now."

The room was every bit as dark as Kenny had said. She propped the door open wide and used the slim ribbon of light flowing from the tower room across the landing. She had been accepting the truth all day, mentally preparing herself, but not for something as stark and certain as this. Her senses reeled as if she'd risen too quickly and found her legs unable to support her. She gripped the door until the weakness passed.

The room must have run forty or fifty feet over the second story of the house. It was partitioned off into two sections with a central hallway running down the middle. At the end of the hallway was a window, but it was shuttered from the outside, closing out the daylight. Each partitioned section had one door opening onto the hallway and a series of windows so small they could not have let in much light, even if the shutters on the one large window had been open. Neither partitioned area had access to direct sunlight or ventilation. Inside each area she saw only rows of crude wooden bunks.

How we must grieve God with our inhumanity! she thought, stricken by the mute reminder of an ugly time in American history. She turned away, thinking of Annie, making record in her diary of the house "bumpin' and creakin' in the night."

Small wonder! Annie was the child who'd nursed crippled animals back to health! She had known the truth—long before her father was charged. It was probably the knowledge clashing with her family loyalty that had caused her such mental distress.

Sorry for the victims and sorry for the girl who'd found herself torn by such a dreadful conflict, Nat wiped away the tears that had sprung to her eyes. She was careful to lock the door behind her, and she stood on the landing a moment, drawing in a lungful of fresh air and trying to restore her composure.

"It's not a pretty sight, is it?"

Jarred, Natalie stepped into the tower room to find Jake, his back to her as he stared out a window. The sight of him squeezed at her aching heart, for he looked much as he had the first day she met him. The same pink shirt stretched across his broad shoulders, narrowing to and tucked into the same white slacks. His dark hair curled just over the collar, his loose, lean look caused the same quick stir in her stomach.

Perhaps it was her silence that turned him around. His blue eyes darkened, and a frown played at his mouth as he saw the tears gilding her lashes.

She swallowed the sob in her throat and forced a steady voice. "It's true, isn't it? Jacob Sutton was guilty

161

of catching those poor people and selling them back into slavery, wasn't he?"

He shoved his hands into his pockets and leaned against the windowsill. Relief was the strongest of his warring emotions and the weight of deception slid from his shoulders. "I've always felt he was. Mother and Harold disagree though."

"How can they be so blind? The room itself is proof enough."

"Maybe you shouldn't have gone in there, Nat."

She misunderstood his concern for her, and her temper flared.

"Don't lecture me on proprieties of being a house guest when not one single person in this house was honest with me! Whether I saw the room or not, I knew. Or did you, like Harold, think I'd gone to *The Daily Journal* office to turn in some kind of slander to hurt his campaign?"

"No. I knew why you went."

"Well, the way things are sizing up, I'm surprised you didn't try to stop me. Isn't that what Harold pays you to do? To keep track of me? To snoop through my manuscript to make certain I'm not telling anything he doesn't want told?"

He was surprised and a new uneasiness crossed his face. "Cut it out, Nat. Harold doesn't pay me anything, and you know it."

"That's right. I forgot. Emotional blackmail is Harold's pet trick. And if Harold chooses, to his advantage, to think Jacob Sutton was innocent, then the book had better say he was innocent, or there isn't going to be a book. Isn't that about the size of it, Jake?"

He shifted away from the windowsill. Her accusations were too strong and he appealed to her sense of fairness. "This isn't like you at all. You've just had a shock, and you need time to adjust. Instead of saying things you'll regret later, just listen a minute.

"Harold and Mother do have a right to their opinion, and their opinion has always been that Jacob was unjustly accused, slandered by his enemies. Mother especially is firm in her belief that the room across the landing was for the housing of the slaves Jacob leased from the South for his saltworks. Distasteful as it was it was at that time within the law, and old Jacob wasn't the only one who made use of it.

"Harold would just as soon the whole matter be forgotten, but you can't fight local legends, and local legends have always painted old Jacob as a man whose ambitions overwhelmed his conscience—which explains Mother's determination to have the book on Jacob accent his good points and leave the rest alone."

"But that isn't history!"

His eyes held hers. "Precisely what I tried to tell you last night. There's probably truth on both sides of the coin."

"Either he did something illegal, or he didn't," she stated flatly. "Besides, even the legal leasing of slave labor was hideously immoral."

"True," Jake agreed. He drew nearer to her. "So what are you going to do now?"

Her head snapped back, her humiliation washing over her again in frightening waves. "You're a fine one to ask me that! I don't have much choice. The book can't go to press as it is. And your mother and Harold aren't going to allow it any other way."

"I don't know, Nat. You could revise it, tell both sides of the story, leave it up to the reader to decide.

Harold wouldn't like it, but I think Mother could adjust once she's made to see any other way threatens your integrity as a writer."

"I'm glad you see that, at least," she said coldly. He made the last step toward her a cautious one.

Then, in his affectionate way, he hooked an arm around the back of her neck and pulled her head against his shoulder, murmuring softly. "Come on, Nat. Don't be like that. I saw from the beginning the truth would put you in a real quandry."

"I found the truth with no help from you," she accused, holding herself stiff and unyielding against his masculine magic.

"Neither did I hinder you," he reminded, his words stirring the loose strands of hair spilling onto her forehead.

"I'm not too sure of that, either." She used her hands as a shield between them, but he was as solid and immovable as a wall.

"Sweetheart, you know I didn't."

His tender endearment tore at her. He could sound so sincere, so convincing! And yet, he'd let her down. He hadn't been truthful with her. And what was love without truth and trust?

"Let me go, Jake," she pleaded, desperately near tears.

"Instead of wasting your energy fighting me, use it constructively. Decide what you're going to do about the book."

"I'm not doing anything about it. I'm going home."

He kissed her temple and laughed with a soft confidence that fired her temper anew. "No, you're not. You aren't a quitter. You'll see this through. I've noticed, however, that your attention wanders when

164

you're writing. So maybe you'll bend to my wishes and not start your revision until after our honeymoon."

"Honeymoon!" The word scattered shock waves of crisscrossing emotions. A day ago, she would have cried for joy. Now her tears were caused by the echo of the conversation she'd overheard in the wee hours of the morning: I don't care how you do it—promise you'll marry her—but keep her quiet.

Something inside her curled up and died. She knew right then Jake was just stringing her along, filling her with ideas for revising the book when in reality he had no more intention of letting her write both sides of the story than Harold or Marianne did.

"You mean it? You'd really marry me?" she tested him in a tight voice that ached in her throat.

"Of course, you silly goose. What did you think?"

She turned her head, and his kiss missed the mark, hitting her ear instead. Her anger built like air filling a balloon to the bursting point. No sacrifice was too great for Harold and his precious political career! Yes, he'd marry her. He might even grow to love her someday, if he ever figured out what the word meant. Feeling suddenly very old and disillusioned, she withdrew from his arms and leveled her hurt at him.

"If the creek went dry, the crops all died, and you were the only man on earth with a loaf of bread, I wouldn't marry you, Jake Brandon. I'll tell you why. Because marriage ought to be based on honesty and trust. I thought honesty was one of your sterling qualities. But you betrayed me! You knew what it meant to me to write this book, and you would have let it go to press a pack of lies. You would have let it stand just to ingratiate yourself with Harold."

"I don't think ingratiate is the right word," he said tersely. "Remember, it was you who urged me to make amends with Harold in the first place."

"Yes, but not at my expense!" she hurled back at him. "It isn't my fault you two fell out over a woman a long time ago, and just for the record, I think she had rotten taste on both counts!"

She whirled away from the sharp hurt that flashed across his face and was gone just as quickly. As she clattered down the stairs, she heard him call after her, "Where are you going?"

"Just where I said—home!"

"All right, if you haven't the gumption to stay here and see it through, to do it the way it ought to be done, then go. But you run away from this one, and you'll be running away from every manuscript that ever gets a little rough going."

She had to bite her tongue to keep from throwing a retort back over her shoulder. Rather, she continued her downward flight, aware he was only a step or two behind her.

"And do you know why, Nat? Because all you want to write about is heroes. You're afraid of disappointment and ugliness. You want perfection in your stories and in life. Maybe you ought to write fairy tales. That ought to suit you just perfectly," he taunted from the doorway of the library as she fled into the parlor.

She gritted her teeth and increased her speed. The tears were salty on her lips and still coming fast. Better to run than to let him see how deeply he'd hurt her.

"So I'm not perfect—sue me!" he called from the bottom of the carpeted stairway.

Halfway up and still running to the sanctuary of her bedroom, she wondered when Hannah and Marianne would be home. Then she could go. She wouldn't ever have to look at him or hear his voice again.

"All right, so I'm sorry. There. Does that make you feel any better?" he asked.

She closed her bedroom door in his face and fumbled with the lock. He was rattling the doorknob by the time she had the lock secured.

"Darn it, Nat, let me in. I want to talk to you."

"I don't want to talk to you. Go away."

"I said I was sorry. You're right. I guess I should have told you. But I was certain you'd find out on your own. Anyway, I did promise Harold I wouldn't say anything."

She scrubbed at her tears with a tissue and answered through the closed door. "You'll have to come up with a better excuse than that. That's grade-school stuff, and you know it!"

"You forget—Harold's confidence is on the grade-school level where I'm concerned."

"I don't want to hear any more about Harold. I'm sick of the whole world's revolving around Harold and his precious career. I don't even think I'll vote for him. A man who can't be honest about his own roots doesn't deserve my vote."

He was quiet a minute. She held her breath, thinking maybe he'd left. Then in a low voice, he wheedled, "Come on, Nat, stop crying and let me in. If you don't, I'm going to have to kick this door in."

"Oh, grow up! Nobody really kicks doors in."

" 'To err is human, to forgive, divine.' "

Easy for him to say just now. But how would he feel if he were the one betrayed? She sniffed into her Kleenex.

" 'Forgive and you will be forgiven.' That's biblical, Nat."

She chewed on her lower lip. Let him quote away until he ran out of quotations! She wasn't letting him in, and he wouldn't dare kick in the door either. That was plain bluff.

Ignoring his rather impressive string of quotations on the subject of forgiveness, she sat cross-legged on her bed, dabbed at her tears, and imagined herself a tour guide showing people through the historical Sutton mansion: "Now watch your step. The lighting is dim. Go up the stairs and to your left. That's where wicked old Jacob kept..."

"All right, enough of this childishness." Jake interrupted her spiteful thoughts with a determination that drew her eyes to the door. "I'm counting to three. Then I'm coming in. One..."

Talk about childish!

"Two, two and a half..."

She let him get to two and three-quarters, then panicked at the thought of his splintering all that beautiful old wood. Bolting off the bed and across the room, she flung open the door.

Jake half walked, half fell into the room. The key in the door fell to the floor. Sheepishly, he shoved it back into his pocket.

"I should have known better than to trust somebody who is so fond of locks and keys." She flounced to the window and turned to glare back at him.

He advanced on her, logical arguments lining his face, but one step away, he stopped short. It was as if he'd taken his first clear look at her since their argument had begun and was shocked by what he saw. His lips parted, but no words came. The cords of his neck tightened as he forced down a hard swallow.

"Nat," he said, self-reproach thickening his voice as he reached out a hand to touch her wet cheek.

Ashamed of her ravaged face, her swollen eyes and red nose, she pivoted away from him to suppress a sob. "Say what you have to say, and then go away and leave me alone."

The room was so quiet the ticking of her alarm clock seemed to mock the pulse of her aching heart. She could feel him behind her, his scrutiny so intent it raised the fine curls on the back of her neck. His hands settled on her upper arms, and his voice was full of tender concern.

"I didn't mean to hurt you. Please don't cry anymore."

Too choked up to answer, she stood, shoulders rounded, fists dashing at her tears. He sounded so loving and gentle, so sincere. And yet she feared his feelings for her only skimmed the surface, made no more than a ripple in his life. Maybe like old Jacob, he suffered a flaw in his character. Maybe his love would never be sufficient to sustain honesty. How she wished he'd told her the truth. How could a promise to Harold mean more to him than her love, her need of him, her respect of what he stood for as a writer?

Her eyes squeezing shut on fresh tears, she tensed as he pulled her against him, his hands linking loosely around her waist. She felt the ragged sigh as it passed through him, heard it against her ear, and read into it a defeat that touched them both.

"Didn't I tell you I had a fatal touch? That I always fail those I care about most? I'm not worth all these tears. You're full of life and promise. I can't blame you for wanting to return home to a family who can love without hurting."

He turned her in his arms then and let her cry it out. He smoothed her hair, gave her gentle pats, the comfort of a friend, not the passion of a lover. And when her tears stopped, he told her he'd explain things to his mother, if she wanted to start home.

Knowing she was so emotionally drained she would only blunder if she stayed and talked to Marianne herself, she accepted his offer.

While he carried her bags and boxes down to her car, she washed away her tears and went to tell Timothy good-bye. He took it casually enough, obviously assuming she'd be back again soon to play baseball with him and dance under the lawn sprinkler.

Jake walked her out to her car, saying little but watching her with sadness in the set of his mouth. She wondered why that should be, but her head was so full of wool from the tears and the trauma of saying good-bye, she didn't stop to consider.

Thinking of Hannah, she unclipped a dainty pin from the collar of her knit shirt and pressed it into Jake's hand. "Give this to Hannah for me, would you? And tell her she's an old dear and I love her."

An odd expression crossed his face as he looked at the pin in his hand. It was only costume jewelry, a tiny cluster of hand-painted violets set in the circular pin.

"Sunshine and violets, spring showers and rainbows," he said softly and leaned near to touch his lips to hers. "Drive carefully, Natalie. And good luck with your writing. You'll make it big one of these days."

She caught her lip between straight white teeth and slid beneath the steering wheel, her ambition in that moment seeming shallow and unsatisfying.

"I left the manuscript on the desk in the library," she said. "It seemed I owed it to your mother. It isn't the bound book she wanted, but maybe she can get it out from time to time and remember old Jacob the way she wants to remember him."

He nodded, seeming to understand she did it as a silent trust, trusting the very ones who'd let her down to make certain the manuscript stayed inside the family circle.

Her gaze met his as she looked at him one last time, trying to seal in the memory of his dark curls dusting his high, proud forehead and the dark fringe of his mustache, the rugged lines of his face so dear and familiar, the creases in his cheeks that could turn to shining dimples, and—best of all—the blue of his eyes, bluer than any summer sky.

Her breath running shallow and fast, she whispered, "Good-bye, Jake."

Her eyes blurred and the taste of tears was bitter. She drove away without looking back.

Chapter Eleven

At home, Natalie found herself forced to give her family hazy explanations of how she'd blown her first truly promising writing job.

Her explanations met with some rather insensitive though good-natured jeers and teasing. Though their hurt was unintentional, Nat remembered Jake's words with bittersweet pain. No family ever loved without hurting.

After her time on her own, she did not feel comfortable living at home, so she combined job hunting with apartment hunting.

Her youngest brother, Al, seemed to sense from her pensive spirit she'd taken a fall and bruised more than her knees and her career hopes. On her third unfruitful day, he made her an offer.

"We were going to keep it a secret a while longer, but I guess I can let the cat out of the bag a little early. Doodle's pregnant and…"

"Pregnant? Al, that's marvelous. Congratulations! Just think, a tiny Doodle underfoot." Laughing over his wife's pet name and overjoyed at his good news, she hugged him hard.

"Anyway," he went on, trying to be businesslike in spite of his proud grin, "she's been feeling under the weather and wouldn't mind taking some time off from the dry-cleaning store. How would you like to fill in for her?"

"Kind though it is of you to ask, I don't know the first thing about the dry-cleaning business."

"All I need is someone to work at the front counter, facing the customers, so to speak. That shouldn't be too tough, should it?"

"I guess not, but are you sure—"

"And during the lulls," he interrupted, "you could work on your writing. Didn't you say you fell behind on that historical saga of yours? Well, this is your perfect chance to catch up!"

"Are you sure you aren't just trying to be nice?" she asked, not wanting to take advantage of his brotherly kindness.

He paid her a crooked grin and cuffed her ears. "You know I'm never nice. You'll find me an impossible landlord."

"Landlord?"

"Of course. I can't afford to pay you the going wage for working in the shop, so I'll make it up to you by letting you have the apartment over the shop rent-free."

It was the most attractive job offer she'd had since returning home, and she accepted.

The apartment was small, so small the window air conditioner churned away at the August heat and actually won the battle at times. Settling in was distracting enough to dull the pain of missing Jake.

Yet there were days when it struck, cutting like the razor-sharp edge of a knife. One of those times was when she received a letter postmarked Sutton Valley.

By the time her fingers pulled the letter from the envelope, they were trembling, and her breath was caught in a secret hope. Marianne, not Jake, was the sender of best wishes among other things.

She wrote:

I am sorry our arrangement did not work out, sorry, too, that you felt it necessary to leave. Yet Jake explained your feelings of betrayal, and I must admit I have not slept well since.

It was not my intention to endanger your integrity as a writer, my dear. And yet, in the end, I can understand your feeling that such was the case. I will not make long explanations or arguments in favor of Jacob, will merely say it has always been my strong feeling he was unjustly accused.

I have enclosed a check to cover your time, for such was our original arrangement. I understand, of course, that the manuscript is never to go to press and will respect your wishes. I hope you will accept payment, for you have more than earned it.

In closing, let me say you brought to our household something far more precious than a book about a man long dead. You brought peace. We all miss you and wish you the best in your career.

Fondly yours,

Marianne Sutton Brandon

So the Brandon world still revolved around Harold, she thought with a twist of bitterness. Jake was still paying his dues, keeping peace at any price.

Hot tears pressed for release. She sank into a rocking chair a few feet in front of the air conditioner, rocking so hard she grew warm in spite of the cool air blowing into her face.

Was she wrong to view it all as she did? To think that in the end, it had come down to a choice, and Jake, from guilt of years past, had chosen his brother over her?

It wasn't like her to consider love a choosing thing. She'd always thought love replenished itself. The more she gave, the more she received. But it didn't appear to work that way in the Brandon household.

And yet Marianne had thanked her for her gift of peace. Nat had lost, but others had gained. Why couldn't she be big enough to pick herself up, dust herself off, and think her personal loss was worth it?

Because I still love him. That was why. The pain of lost love throbbed in the back of her head like a headache from which there was no relief.

She closed her eyes, though in her heart she didn't feel like praying. It seemed as if her prayers bounced around inside and never reached the throne of God.

No! she reminded herself sternly. Her faith was based not on feeling but on the love of Christ. She prayed the prayer of Christ, "...*not as I will, but as you will.*"

As the days passed, she continued to pray, confused prayers sometimes, but prayers all the same. She could not have said when the bitter feeling left her, when she felt for scars and realized there were none.

All she knew was that she felt older and wiser and was writing better than she'd ever written before. If that was the price she had to pay—loving Jake with a love that saw no end—then maybe it was worth it.

She did not return Marianne's check, for she had no wish to insult her. Neither did she feel right cashing it. So it was shuffled under her typewriter and lay there collecting erasure crumbs.

More mail came from Sutton Valley. First, a stiff little note from Hannah, thanking her for the pin and scolding her for running off without a word. Then, a sweet card from Timothy saying he'd hit a home run the last little league game and asking when she was coming back.

The third week in August when she had all but given up hope, she heard from Jake. It was a postcard, unsigned, with a simple three-word message: "I miss you."

Clutching it to her, she called to her brother in the back of the shop. "I'm going to take a short coffee break, okay?"

He grumbled something less than poetic back at her, but it only served to hasten her departure. Dashing up the back stairs, her heart filling with hope renewed, she whispered, "Thank you, Lord."

For in that moment nothing could have been sweeter than to hold in her hand the card he'd chosen from a rack of others. It would provoke such memories, no signature was necessary.

The picture postcard was a night scene, a grove of trees keeping silent watch in the background while a buck and a doe grazed beneath a butterscotch moon. She turned the card over to study the scrawl and the postmark. *Pathetic way for a grown woman to act,* she thought and laughed at herself.

So what now? Her heart raced. Did she pick up the phone, call him, tell him she missed him, too—far, far, more than mere words could express? No, she knew even as the temptation stole over her that she couldn't. The sound of his voice would steal every word from her tongue. She'd stammer and perspire and maybe even lose her nerve and hang up.

Rather, she'd write something quick and clever and breezily noncommittal.

When Al called her from downstairs to tell her her coffee break was over, she tucked a butterscotch candy in an envelope and settled for a simple signature of truth: "Love, Natalie."

There.

When the mailbox on the corner had swallowed her letter, misgivings rushed in. Why had she been so swift to respond? Nothing had changed. He'd still let her down, danced to Harold's tune. Nothing had changed.

Or had it? She raced back to the shop, thoughts flying as fast as her feet. Something *had* changed, something inside of her. She'd had time to step back and feel what had happened between them. She'd had time to know the heavy ache of being without him. She'd had time to acknowledge her part in the misunderstanding.

She squirmed a bit inside. Her actions had bordered on self-centeredness. For despite what Jake had or had not done, she'd felt overly anxious, threatened even by his renewed ties with his brother, ties she'd initially encouraged! She had read disloyalty to herself into his loyalty to Harold.

How sanctimonious of her to think that because Jake had let her down he did not know how to love. Maybe it was *she* who needed the lesson in love. She slowed her steps and turned into the shop hoping "I miss you" was another way of saying "I love you."

If a second chance came her way, she would know how to handle it.

Not knowing when or how or even *if* an answer would come made waiting an agony. She reasoned it would take her letter a day, two at the most, to reach him. Her heart leaped each time the phone rang, only to sink into the mire of disappointment when the voice on the other end wasn't his.

She kept herself busy. Every moment she wasn't eating or sleeping, or working in the shop, she was writing. Even then, the total concentration her writing required was fractured by daydreams creeping in slippered feet, worries more heavily shod, and occasionally the shrill ring of the phone.

In fact, Nat recalled years that had passed more swiftly than the three days after she posted her letter to Jake.

She thought it was the doorbell at first, irritatingly persistent in rousing her from an exhausted sleep. But the rhythm was more regular. The phone! Now who in the world would call so late?

Shaking off the last holds of sleep, she leaped out of bed and sprinted out to the living room by the light leaking through the curtains from the streetlights outside her windows.

One step away from the phone, she ran her toe against the skirt-concealed leg of the sofa. Holding back a yelp of pain, she reached for the phone with one hand, her poor mangled toe with the other, and rolled onto the sofa, hissing, "Hello?" through set teeth.

There was an empty pause, then an uneasy chuckle. "Maybe I better call back at a more reasonable hour.

That wasn't the most cordial greeting I've ever heard."

Sleep gone, pain forgotten, hope singing through her veins, she said with an honesty that made him laugh, "I stubbed my toe."

"I should have called earlier..."

"No, it was my fault," she rushed in. "I didn't turn on any lights, just ran through two rooms straight into the sofa leg."

"...but I just got around to reading my mail. I've been gone a couple of days." He chuckled again, as if it had just registered what she'd done. "No lights, huh? You must have been in a hurry. Should I be flattered?"

"I didn't know it was you," she began, then decided to dispense with the coy pretense. No hurt could be worse than losing him. Now, to see if she could win him back...

"But I was hoping it was," she finished softly.

"I *am* flattered."

At the sound of his laughter, vulnerability rushed in. "Don't tease," she pleaded, gripping the phone hard. "I've been miserable."

"Me, too."

They were the dearest words! Her eyes filled with unexpected tears. "Really?"

"Of course, really. What did you think? That I'd go on my merrily whistling way when you told me you wouldn't marry me if I were..."

"Don't," she interrupted, for the injured pride in his voice hurt her. "Don't remind me what I said. I was childish and horrid, and I'm sorry. It was just that...I don't know, Jake. Sometimes we don't communicate too well, do we?"

"Let's try it without words. That is, if you'll have dinner with me tomorrow."

Having made the call, he now seemed impatient to be done with it. He and Harold planned to spend the day in Springfield at the State Fair. He'd drive on up to Lincoln and take her out to dinner. Since she knew the town, she would make reservations.

She hung up the phone, dealing with warring emotions. Such joy had filled her at the sound of his voice. And at first, he'd seemed relaxed, at ease, glad to hear her voice, too. But then there had been a subtle change in him. What was it she'd said to bring about that change? Despite how many times she reran the conversation through her head, she could not pin it down.

Would she ever understand him? Possibly not, but given the chance, she was willing to dedicate her life to it.

Al looked terribly annoyed. "You just got here! What do you mean you want the day off?"

Determined, Nat stood her ground. "Al, you've been wonderful to me and I shouldn't be asking favors, but even if I stayed, my mind wouldn't be on my work today. So how about it? Is Doodle feeling well enough to come in? Just for today, I promise."

His scowl deepened. "I'm seriously considering taking you off my Christmas list."

Which meant, against his better judgment, he was going to give in. Natalie grinned. "You do that. Just give me the day off."

"Would it be prying if I asked what you plan to do with it?"

"Yes. But I'll tell you anyway. I'm going to the State Fair."

Sharp with disgust, he said, "Sometimes I really worry about you, Nat."

"Okay, okay, so I met this guy. He's kind of special, and he's going to be at the fair today. I thought I'd surprise him."

Defeated, he waved her away. "I give up. Just go. Oh, and Nat? Bring Doodle back a box of that saltwater taffy, would you?"

She ran back and hugged him. "You're a terrific brother and I'll be forever grateful."

"Yeah, yeah," he said. The sullen twist of his mouth didn't dampen her spirits in the least. For she had decided she could not wait until evening to see Jake again.

She bought a new dress, a cotton-candy pink at a price she couldn't afford, but she giggled as she wrote out the check and went on to buy sandals to match. Her hair was freshly shampooed and floating around her face and shoulders like a toasted marshmallow cloud. And her car had a full tank of gas. She nosed it down the southbound lane of the interstate highway, her determination steady.

It had been years since she had been to the State Fair. But the sights and sounds were as familiar as yesterday. As were the smells. Tom Thumb doughnuts hot out of the fat, popcorn, and thick steak sandwiches cooked over huge charcoal grills all vied for her attention, but she weakened only once and that was in the dairy building where the Butter Cow drew the crowd and the cream puffs sent them happily on their way.

Walking in the tracks of show animals, she kept one eye on the ground as she licked the last of the whipped cream from her fingers and wondered where to start looking for Harold's campaign booth.

A map of the grounds narrowed down the possibilities. After a few wrong turns, she wound up in the right tent by the process of elimination.

The tent was swarming with politicians. It was Governor's Day, so naturally all political factions were warring for attention.

She spotted Harold first, and then she saw him. Jake was a few steps farther on bent over a table, cheerfully forging Harold's autograph for a couple of wide-eyed schoolgirls. For a moment, she was as star-struck as the big-eyed teens with the frivolous giggles.

Jake was casually clad in an attractive gray shirt with blue stripes running through. The short sleeves revealed hard brown muscle. Gray dress slacks were well-suited to his narrow waist and trim hips. Even with fans roaring all around the tent was hot, and perspiration beaded his brow, dampening the dark curls that strayed there. The makings of a smile hovered beneath his mustache, and fine lines fanned out from his eyes as he bade the two girls farewell.

Fighting a sudden bout of shyness, Nat sidled up to the table strewn with buttons and pencils and paper hats. Her heart in her mouth, she asked, "Could I interest you in a ride on the double Ferris wheel?"

His startling blue eyes flashed over her, his initial surprise giving way to a warm smile. "Hello, Nat. What brings you here?"

"I've come to see the sights, of course. Why should you and Harold have all the fun, hopping from fair to fair?" she said with practiced carelessness.

Ripples ran through her as he reached across the table that kept them apart and captured her chin. He softly accused, "Liar. Now tell me the truth."

Why didn't he show some sign of elation instead of

leaving her dangling in midair? Was he glad to see her, or was she making a nuisance of herself, stealing time from his campaigning efforts for Harold?

Uncertain, she moistened her lips, wordlessly pleading for a sign. A slow smile stole across his face, deepening his dimples, illuminating his eyes. With a finger pleasantly rough, he traced the fullness of her mouth.

"Say it, and I'll clock out of this canvas oven. I'll buy you a steak sandwich and a lemonade shake-up, and we'll find somewhere quiet to talk."

"What shall I say?"

Her heart thrashed about as he leaned nearer, his mouth only a hairsbreadth away.

"That you love me and couldn't wait until evening to tell me so."

"And for that, I get a steak sandwich and a lemonade?" she asked, her heart leaping from uncertainty to the pinnacle of her hopes.

"For that, you get me." He stroked her lips with his own, stirring such a radiant glow she forgot the crowds pushing past, the table between them and all her inhibitions.

"All right, then. I love you…and evening seemed forever."

For one enchanted moment, life was his kiss, the clean male scent of him, and the giddy reel of her heart. Their quarrels and pain no longer mattered. Their love would endure.

Harold brought them back to earth. Clearing his throat, he noted in dry tones, "I've heard of kissing babies for a vote, but don't you think you're carrying it a bit too far, Jake?" Reluctantly, Jake let her go, but only long enough to circle the table. Clasping her hand firmly in his, he tossed at Harold, "We're off. See you later."

"Now wait a second," Harold blustered. "You promised to help out today, Jake. Hey, come back here, you two!"

They paused only long enough for Harold to pin a "Vote for Brandon" button to Nat's collar and grumble, "You might as well do some advertising."

"Come on, Nat, before he slaps a bumper sticker across your backside." Jake pulled her along, chuckling at the color that rose to her cheeks.

"Where are you headed in case I need to find you?" Harold asked.

"First to Sleepy Hollow," Jake called back. "We're going to ride the double Ferris wheel and the roller coaster, then get lost in the tunnel of love."

Looking as if he wished he hadn't asked, Harold shook his head and turned away. Jake grinned and squeezed her hand. "Sometimes, Harold's a bit of a stuffed shirt, isn't he?"

Nat smothered a laugh. "You promised me a steak sandwich and lemonade."

"After the rides. I don't want to risk kissing a sick woman at the top of the double Ferris wheel."

"And then?"

A warning glittered in his blue eyes. "And then I'm going to ask you one more time to marry me, so don't blow it."

She laughed and promised, "I won't."

Half a dozen rides, a steak lunch, and an accepted proposal later, they swung along hand in hand through the Conservation Area where tall prairie grass and a log cabin replica brought old Jacob to mind.

"You know, Jake, I've given it a lot of thought, and I

think I know where I went wrong on the book project."

"*Accepting* the project is where you went wrong," he said, catching a lock of her hair and smoothing it back from her face.

"Maybe. But since I did accept, I hate the unfinished feeling that lingers. It's just that I realize now I can't do it within the confines of strict fact. I'm not a historian."

"No, I tried to tell you that once."

"And I got mad. Probably because I sensed you were more right than wrong. So I'm going to try it again. Only this time, I'm going to do it the only way I know how."

"Which is?"

She listened to the dry rustling sound of the breeze snaking through the tall grasses. It was a sound she could capture in her novel. "I'll write it as a historical novel. Not strictly the way it was, but the way it might have been."

"And old Jacob? Will he come off guilty or innocent?"

She drew her hand from his and linked an arm around his lean waist. Wondering herself just how old Jacob would come out, she tilted her head back and did her best to look mysterious.

"If I told you that, you wouldn't read the book."

He kissed her, chuckled softly, and kissed her again.

Forever Romances are inspirational romances designed to bring you a joyful, heart-lifting reading experience. If you would like more information about joining our Forever Romance book series, please write to us:

Guideposts Customer Service
39 Seminary Hill Road
Carmel, NY 10512

Forever Romances are chosen by the same staff that prepares *Guideposts,* a monthly magazine filled with true stories of people's adventures in faith. *Guideposts* is not sold on the newsstand. It's available by subscription only. And subscribing is easy. Write to the address above and you can begin reading *Guideposts* soon. When you subscribe, each month you can count on receiving exciting new evidence of God's Presence, His Guidance and His limitless love for all of us.

G